I0603672

BELLETRISIC
PRESS

FORBIDDEN

To learn more about the author, visit his
YouTube channel: Onyxe Blade

To learn more about the FORBIDDEN series,
check out: DarkOnyxe.blogspot.com

ONYXE BLADE

BELLETRISTIC PRESS
NEW YORK

BELLETRISIC
PRESS

Belletristic Press, LLC
Brooklyn, NY 11235
www.belletristicpress.com

PUBLISHER'S NOTE

This book is a work of fiction. Names, characters, places, and incidents are either products of the author's imagination or are used fictitiously. Any resemblance to actual events or locales or persons, living or dead, is entirely coincidental.

First BELLETRISTIC PRESS Edition 2021
Belletristic Press colophon and design
are trademarks of Belletristic Press, LLC
Printed in the United States of America

Library of Congress Cataloging-in-Publication Data on file

ISBN 978-0-9796594-7-8

10 9 8 7 6 5 4 3 2 1

Cover Design by Aron Knight

*Dedicated to the everlasting loving memory of
my nephew,*

Aisyn Zade Emerson-Gonzalez

September 21, 2016 – September 11, 2021

Forever Loved

Hey buddy,

I'm writing to you because I can no longer tell you this in person. I loved you so much from the very moment I laid eyes on you until Jehovah took you to Heaven to be with Him. I truly wish you were still here, so I could show you my book in person, Aisyn. I swear you were one of the best parts of my life for the nearly five years that I was so lucky to call you my nephew. I don't want to move forward nor will I truly ever. As long as I breathe, there will never be a day when I do not think about you. I deeply wanted to take a picture of you holding my book once it was released. It would've been two of my greatest achievements in one beautiful picture. Sadly, even with all the knowledge I have gained over my years of existence, I didn't know our time together would end so soon, and the way that it did.

I'm so angry that you aren't here with me anymore, but I guess this is for the best. I passionately don't feel that way, and I never will. At least, I know you're in a better place now. I will love you always and forever, Aisyn, and I look forward to the day we meet again, my fellow Virgo amigo.

Love you forever,

Uncle Onyxe

ACKNOWLEDGMENTS

To my mother, Gilda Celestin, for being the greatest mother alive, and always loving me even when I didn't love myself. My best friend, Mitchel Taylor, for inspiring me to be my most authentic self. Jennifer Williams for being a true and loving friend to me. Elisa and Ana Lopez for their constant support and the boundless humor they bring to my life. My Godson, Antonio Clark, for making me so proud as you continue to grow into a wonderful young adult. To my grandmother, Bedena Emerson, for being the best Granny. Much love to my siblings, Tynann, Javyn, and Fahryn-Zade, along with family and friends who have shaped me into the man I am today. And last but most important, my nephew, Aisyn Zade Emerson-Gonzalez. I love you so, so much and I am thankful to have such a bundle of joy as my nephew. I love you so very much, and I look forward to the amazing person you will become.

PUBLISHER'S NOTE:

Onyxe wrote his Acknowledgments prior to the tragic loss of his beloved nephew, Aisyn. He later dedicated this novel to Aisyn. As publisher, Belletristic Press deemed it fitting to leave Onyxe's Acknowledgments intact as he originally intended.

1

Another Day, Another Tragedy

24 HOURS AGO

SOMEWHERE in a secret location hidden within Eket, Nigeria, a young man named Trevyn Aliyu, the son and only child of the Queen of Nigeria, Adama Aliyu, has been kidnapped. Seized with him were his friends, Jamaal and Alimi. Prior to finding himself constrained to a lab table, Trevyn remembered Alimi, Jamaal, and himself playing in a park not too far from his favorite mall. Despite being unable to free himself from his captors, Trevyn continued resisting to no avail.

Entering the room with him were three men with a sinister air surrounding them. Trevyn noticed that neither Jamaal nor Alimi was in the room with him, and began shouting out their names. Neither of his friends answered him. All three kidnappers, wearing lab coats, approached Trevyn. There were two white males and a black male, who appeared to be the leader of the devious trio. Angry and afraid of his circumstances and the whereabouts of his friends, Trevyn learned of his terrifying situation and the fate of his friends from the leader of the lab coats.

Dr. Ezekiel: Greetings, Prince Aliyu, you're probably wondering why my colleague twins, doctors Richard and Alec Miles, have chosen your friends and you. It's quite simple: My colleagues and I plan to use you three for an experiment we call *Project Demon Slayer.* Unfortunately, unlike your friends, only you managed to survive the first part of the experiment. However, before you get upset with us, blame your mother, Queen Aliyu, for removing the restrictions that allowed demons into Nigeria.

Dr. Richard Miles: Demons are a threat to mankind's survival, and should never be welcomed with open arms just because a small percentage of them are deemed humane enough to live amongst us. Some of them even have the nerve to breed with us humans. That doesn't make them any less of an abomination that we, as a whole, need to exterminate from existence.

Dr. Ezekiel: Fortunately, my colleagues and I have discovered a forbidden technique that turns mortals into angel-like beings; giving them powers equivalent to angels in the Heavens, which have forsaken us many centuries ago, and left us to deal with the demon plight ourselves. Even with all the magic and technology in the world, none of that would be enough should demons ever turn on us as a collective. Therefore, we must act now before it's too late for us. Luckily, we have the means to create Artificial Holy Warriors...should they survive the experimentation, of course. That gives us the manpower to fight back against the demons. Either driving them all back to the Underworld or better yet, sending them into extinction. Now that you know our intentions, let us proceed with the experiment.

Trevyn: Why my friends! Why me! My mother is a gracious Queen, and everything she does is with wise intentions. Her decision to lift the restrictions had nothing to do with her friendship with the King of Mayland. I'm so fucking mad you fucking people killed my friends. Why did you have to do this to us!

Dr. Ezekiel: Nothing personal...your friends and you were at the right place at the wrong time. As for whatever pathetic reason your mother may have for removing the restrictions for demons in Nigeria, those actions endanger my people and I will not stand for it. Once this is all said and done, I will prove to be the leader that Nigeria desperately needs. Now prepare yourself for the next step in becoming our artificial angel.

Earlier in her homeland of Babylon within the Underworld, Hellin enjoyed breakfast with her foster sister and best friend, Orsela. While eating their breakfast the girls were interrupted by Ozzy, one of the many servants of Babylon. Without the man ever saying a single word, the girls stopped eating and followed him. They knew that he was sent by Queen Othello to give them yet another assignment. Standing before their mother, who sat on her throne, Hellin and Orsela waited as Othello began speaking.

Othello: Greetings, girls, so sorry to disturb your breakfast, but Mama has work for you two lovelies.

Orsela: Greetings, your Majesty, it's never a problem stopping our scrumptious breakfast to come and listen to you.

Othello: Was that sarcasm, Orsela?

Orsela: ...Oh no, your Majesty, I was just...

Hellin: Do shut up, Orsela! Mother, please don't tell me we're going to Mayland?

Othello: Okay, you're not going to Mayland.

Hellin: Shit! What does that asshole, Onyx, want now?

Othello: There was an incident in Nigeria. Three children went missing.

Orsela: OMG that's awful!

Hellin: So? People go missing all the time. How the fuck does that concern us? Let alone require that dickwad to need us to get involved?

Othello: Well, Daughter, if you let me talk, I will explain everything in detail as to why this particular situation is different from your usual missing person. Two of the missing children are commoners, but the third missing child is the son of Nigeria's current ruler, Queen Aliyu, whom, as you two should already know, is an ally of Onyx. Therefore, Onyx has taken personal interest in finding out what happened to Prince Aliyu. That is, if the boy is still alive since his two friends' bodies were found floating in the Imo River just a few hours ago.

Orsela: This is absolutely awful news. Poor Prince Aliyu and those dead friends of his. I truly hope he is still alive.

Hellin: So, let me guess: Whoever had the fucking nerve to kidnap Queen Aliyu's son, Onyx wants us to go to Nigeria and investigate his disappearance and find his captors.

Othello: Obviously, Daughter, but I can't simply open a portal to Nigeria, and you two go off and investigate. While Nigeria has only recently become more welcoming of demons, one of their laws still prevents demons from opening a portal into their country. That's why you two will first go visit The Naked King, aka: Onyx, at his kingdom in the Royal Lands. Speak with him to further under-stand the situation before he sends you off to investigate. Now, ladies, let me go fetch Madame Xi and have her open a portal into the Royal Lands for you. Mama has yet another meeting with her fellow Demon Lords to attend.

Othello stepped off her throne and walked over to Hellin and Orsela. She gave Hellin a kiss on the forehead then patted Orsela's head and neatened up her hair in the process. Othello then walked away from her daughters and prepared to attend her meeting. Hellin and Orsela went off to find Madame Xi and got ready to go see King Onyx once again.

2

This F*cking Guy Again

A PORTAL opened right into Borden, the capital of the Royal Lands and the very location of Mayland's current King, Onyx, and where all past kings and queens who ruled before him had resided. Hellin and Orsela were immediately greeted by their friend and assigned Rider, Mariah, who gleefully expected their arrival while sitting atop her pink and goldenrod colored horse, Mozzarella. Orsela and Mariah had a friendly chat while Hellin went straight inside the carriage and waited for Mariah to take them to King Onyx's castle. Hellin irritatedly watched as Mariah and Orsela continued flapping their gums before she angrily alerted both women that they had somewhere to be. The two women apologized before Orsela joined Hellin, as Mariah ordered Mozzarella to take them to meet Onyx.

Twenty minutes later, the girls arrived at the entrance of Onyx's castle where two guards in magical armor stood before the castle door. Recognizing the women immediately, the guards opened the door without hesitation. Mariah waved goodbye to Hellin and Orsela. They waved back before entering the castle.

Inside the castle, Hellin and Orsela, as expected, found themselves surrounded by Onyx's various servants and highly trained guards. The girls were then greeted by Yura Mikan, better known as the right-hand woman of King Onyx. She walked them to the dining room where they were seated around several other guards with Onyx's best friend and right-hand man, James Del Soto, and his daughter, Anna, sitting across from them. An empty creamy pink and amethyst-jeweled dining chair was placed between James and Anna. The very chair where the King himself sits to eat. At the dinner table was a wonderful array of food for everyone to enjoy, made by the devoted chefs of the King. Unable to finish her breakfast earlier in Babylon, Orsela treated herself to a plate of watermelon, bourbon salmon, cranberry mac and cheese, empanadas, and a glass of pineapple soda.

Meanwhile, Hellin and Anna gave each other dirty looks as both women tried to ignore their demonic instincts to fight each other; especially since Hellin was there on a mission and not about to have a showdown with one of her many rivals. James noticed the tension between Hellin and his daughter, but remained quiet in hopes of not escalating the situation; noting the last time they fought, his daughter lost the match. Eventually, everyone just started eating as they waited for the loving but late king to arrive.

King Onyx appeared from around the corner wearing his signature see-through house robe with a purple thong covering his genitals, which is the reason he'd been given the nickname The Naked King. The King appeared with a smile brighter than the sun as he greeted everyone good morning. Taking his seat between James and Anna, Onyx grabbed a bowl of mixed fruit and gobbled it down.

While everyone enjoyed their breakfast and chatted friendly with one another, Hellin found herself staring at Onyx once again. It's not like she hasn't met him over a thousand times since her mother introduced them to each other over two hundred years ago. She was horrified that Mayland's current king looked so much like her or worse, she looked so much like him; minus the features that Hellin inherited from her mother. It was like looking into a mirror whenever she saw Onyx. Worse still, whenever she was around him, Hellin couldn't help but feel incomplete. Ever since their first encounter, Hellin tried to figure out her connection to him through her mother, to no avail. Eventually, she grew to hate him to the point of wanting to kill him. However, her mother, Othello, a much stronger telepath, became aware of her feelings toward him. Othello warned her daughter if she ever made an attempt on Onyx's life that the consequences would be dire. Therefore, she refrained from attempting to kill Onyx, but despised him nonetheless.

Unfortunately, the same could not be said for Onyx who actually admired Hellin and viewed her as a friend, despite her callous behavior towards him. He was never once remotely curious as to why one of the princesses of Babylon looked so much like him. He was just happy to have a friend in the Underworld he could always count on; even if he was unaware of how much she didn't want to be bothered. While today would not be the day she got to the bottom of her connection to the King, Hellin and Orsela did not come to eat mortal food and chit chat with Onyx at his castle residence. They were there to learn about the disappearance of Prince Aliyu.

Hellin: So, Onyx, you want to get to the fucking reason you had my mother send Orsela and myself to you yet again?

Onyx: Oh, how loving and direct as ever, Hellin. I, unfortunately, need Orsela and you to go to Nigeria and find out what happened to my friend Queen Aliyu's son, Trevyn. Two of his friends were found dead floating in the Imo River, and I fear Trevyn's fate may be no different. Nonetheless, I want the two of you to go to Nigeria and find out who may have taken him.

Hellin: That's if his captors haven't left Nigeria by now.

Onyx: That's a possibility but since the incident, Queen Aliyu has placed Nigeria on lockdown. No one gets in or out without her knowing.

James: Plus, only fools would risk trying to dip out of Nigeria with everything that's going on.

Anna: Unless they are teleporters, of course.

Onyx: Queen Aliyu already had her servant place a powerful anti-teleportation spell, so that won't work. Anyone who even attempts to teleport in or out of Nigeria would be exposed on the spot. The anti-teleportation spell turns the teleporter's skin olive green and causes them to vomit every thirty minutes. Also, since there are no Orcs in Nigeria, it will be easy to spot an olive-skinned Sage who tried to use any form of teleportation. And before you mention any olive-skinned demons already in Nigeria, Queen Aliyu made certain that none of demons currently residing there are that skin color.

Orsela: Sounds like Queen Aliyu took exceptional measures to make things hard for her son's captors.

Anna: As she should. Those fuckers who kidnapped Trevyn must be found. It's just too bad I have my own assignment, so I can't join you in hunting those bastards down.

Hellin: And what a relief it is to not have you tagging along.

Anna: Oh, Hellin, as if I want to be around you any more than necessary.

Onyx: Ladies, please, this is not the time. The two of you can rematch another time. Right now, we have more important matters at hand. As you should already be aware, if your mother briefed the two of you, Nigeria has placed an anti-portal rule for demons coming to their country. Therefore, I cannot simply open a portal in Nigeria for you two. Even with our friendship, Queen Aliyu must keep her rules in place.

Hellin: Then how are we going to get to Nigeria? Hunt down a dragon and force it to fly us there or do you fucking expect us to travel there on foot? If that cunt hopes to see her son alive, she needs to lift that fucking rule of hers even if it's temporarily.

Onyx: In a perfect world that would be the case, but that would risk giving Trevyn's captors and his friends' murderers a chance to escape. Fortunately, I have already figured out a way for you two to get to Nigeria without having to capture a dragon, of course. However, you two will have to go to Texas first in order to meet your final partner for this mission. Once you two have done that, you will then be introduced to a Sage who is capable of teleporting the three of you to Cameroon. From there, the three of you will travel the traditional way to Nigeria.

Orsela: Oh wow, Onyx, you are so fucking awesome! That is such a well thought out plan. But who are we going to meet up with in Texas?

Hellin: Are you fucking kidding, Orsela? There's only one Sage we know in Texas that we worked with a few times before... unfortunately.

Orsela:...OMG, we're going to see August!

Hellin: Fuck! Why do we need August tagging along with us, Onyx?

Onyx: Hey, August is awesome! And besides, this mission is going to require at least one of you to be human. Having two demons roaming around Nigeria, even at Queen Aliyu's request, is going to raise a lot of eyebrows. At least if one of you is human, it makes things a lot better.

Hellin: August isn't even fully human. Isn't he like part fairy after his near-death experience years prior to meeting Orsela and me?

Onyx: August has fairy blood in him but he is still classified as human, and is therefore qualified. Now that we're all caught up, time I get you ladies on your way.

Hellin: Will you at least open a portal for us to enter Texas?

Onyx: That won't be a problem. But in order to give August and his crew time to complete their current assignment, I'm going to instead open a portal to Blue Jay City.

From there, Orsela and you will catch the bullet train at the Steel White station and head to Texas. I'm certain by then August will be ready to journey with the two of you.

Hellin: Oh, he better be, your Highness!

The servants came to collect the plates from the table as Yura entered the dining room. The party of five all rose from their seats. The six of them headed to Onyx's garden located behind his castle. Onyx created a portal for Hellin and Orsela to enter into Blue Jay City. Onyx and his Royal Guards bade the ladies farewell as they stepped into the portal.

Meanwhile, at an undisclosed location in Rogue Town, one of the seedier states within the country of Mayland, there was a meeting between a vanilla-skinned woman named Love and a mysterious man wearing an ebony demon mask with ebony gloves and dressed in a burgundy suit. Love stood before him with her pale skin and strawberry blonde hair with small streaks of pink, cerulean, and lime green dye. She wore a black catsuit with the zipper pulled down past her belly button. She stared at the man with her cold but beautiful blue eyes. While caressing the scar around her neck, she awaited his commands.

Mysterious Man: You know why I asked you to meet me here, Ms. Love?

Love: Other than killing someone, not really. Unless, of course, that someone is you.

Love looked at the man with murder in her eyes.

Mysterious Man: You're a very capable assassin despite having no magic, but do not push your luck, Ms. Love. Fortunately for you, I do have someone I want you to kill for me. A former colleague of mine by the name of Nathaniel Ezekiel betrayed me. While I feel no need to go into details with you, understand, his actions cannot go un-punished. Through reliable intel, I've discovered he's hiding somewhere in Nigeria. Fitting...since that's where he's from. I guess the fool thought he would be safest in his homeland from my wrath. He's clearly unaware of how deep my connections run in the Dark Society.

Love: Well, I don't care about the details either...as long as the job pays well. However, it's going to be a pain in the ass to travel all the way from Mayland to Nigeria. It's not like

I'm some Sage or demon who can just create a portal there. Even if I were, if the rumors I hear are true, Queen Aliyu has her country on lockdown. Nonetheless, a job is a job, so I'll find a way in...one way or another.

Mysterious Man: It is indeed true that Queen Aliyu has Nigeria locked down, but you need not sweat the details. I know people who can get you close enough to Nigeria and you can take it from there. All I ask is for one thing in return, Ms. Love...well two, actually.

Love: And that would be?

Mysterious Man: Do not betray me...and bring me Ezekiel's brain!

3

Fight to Texas

SHORTLY after walking through the portal, Hellin and Orsela arrived in Blue Jay City. The two women immediately headed to the BJ45 bus stop. They needed to reach the Steel White train station the quickest way possible without having to find a Rider, since Mariah wasn't available in Blue Jay City to drop them off herself. They purchased their tickets then boarded the bullet train, which made limited stops. Moving towards the back of the train, Hellin took the seat next to the window as Orsela sat beside her on the aisle seat. Other passengers boarded the train, the majority of them were human and one Cambion: a half human and half demon being.

Everything was going smoothly despite Hellin having a bad vibe that she could not quite explain. Perhaps it was just her usual pessimism or maybe she sensed a danger that had yet to reveal itself. Before the train pulled out, a tall, pale-skinned man dressed in a beige suit came aboard. He wore brown slacks, dark sunglasses, and an expensive silver watch on his right arm. He had spiky black hair with yellow tips, and he carried a beige hat that matched his suit.

The man appeared to be a regular civilian to the average person, but both Hellin and Orsela were aware of the man's true identity. The man spotted the two women and headed towards them. Taking the available seat across from them, the man began to speak.

Kthanid: Hey, it's been a while since I last saw you ladies. How's everything going for you two?

Orsela: It's good to see you as well, Kthanid. It must have been about two years since we last saw you back in Rogue Town.

Hellin: What in the world are you doing on this train, alien?

Kthanid: I see you're still as lovely as ever, Hellin.

Hellin: Do I need to take a peek into your fucking mind or will you share your reason for being here willingly?

Kthanid: You're a powerful telepath, Ms. Strongs, but I wouldn't advise taking a peek into my mind right about now. I have been having a rather complicated past few days. The less you know, the better. I'm simply trying to get to Texas to enjoy the carnival later this evening.

Orsela: So, is your brother still trying to have you eliminated?

Kthanid: When is he not, Orsela? Thankfully, I have avoided that bastard for quite some time. I just wish I could say the same for some of his crazy disciples. Fortunately, life has been relatively peaceful for me as of late.

Hellin: Let's hope it stays that way until we part ways, alien. Orsela and I have business to tend to in Texas, so we would like to get there without any bullshit.

Kthanid: Not that it matters to me, but I assume you two are aware that the Prince of Nigeria is currently missing?

Hellin: Oh, we know. That's why we need to get to Texas as soon as possible. Now, either talk to Orsela or be quiet. The sooner we part ways, the better.

Kthanid: Orsela makes for much better conversation anyway, Princess of Babylon.

The bullet train hurried from Blue Jay City to Texas as passengers did things from chatting, listening to music on various devices, reading a book, or just looking outside the window in silence. An hour passed as the train drew closer to its destination. Then, just as Hellin had sensed a malicious presence on the train, a green tentacle broke through the roof of the train and grabbed Kthanid around his neck. Kthanid was pulled out of the train as everyone, besides Hellin and Orsela, screamed in terror.

Hellin: I fucking knew it! Trouble follows that fucking man everywhere.

Orsela: Hellin, now is not the time. I'll calm down the passengers with the help of Nox Valerie. Meanwhile, go save Kthanid from whatever grabbed him out the train.

Hellin glared at Orsela before springing out of the train from the hole created by the tentacle. Standing on the roof of the train, Hellin found herself facing a man dressed in a black suit that looked like a cross between a ninja and a dominatrix. One of his hands appeared normal while the other was a long green tentacle holding Kthanid hostage. The mysterious man immediately turned his attention to Hellin.

Tentacle Arm Assailant: Go back inside the train, woman! My business is with him and him alone!

Hellin: I would love nothing more than to go back inside the fucking train but thanks to you, that's out of the question. However, if you let go of the alien and fuck off, I'll pretend none of this ever happened. Otherwise, I'll make you wish you never met me.

Tentacle Arm Assailant: You dare threaten me, woman? Seems you don't value your life. I'm going to make you regret sticking your nose in my business...

(((Poison Shot)))

From his free hand the Tentacle Arm Assailant shot out a greyish-purple energy blast towards Hellin. Using her demon reflexes, Hellin performed a hands-free cartwheel and dodged the attack. The Assailant looked at her in shock and quickly realized the woman before him was no regular woman.

Tentacle Arm Assailant: ...You're a demon! I should've known no ordinary woman would dare stand against me. It doesn't matter. I have killed your kind before in battle, and you will be no different.

Hellin: If you mistake me for your run-of-the-mill demon, you're in for a rude fucking awakening.

Tentacle Arm Assailant: I can't fight this wench while holding you hostage, traitor! I'll finish you off once I eliminate her! However, I'll make sure you don't attempt to escape by paralyzing you first.

Hellin: Think again, asshole!

Before the Tentacle Arm Assailant could release a toxin from his arm to paralyze the captured Kthanid, Hellin used her telepathy to take over the alien's mind. She forced him to release Kthanid from his grasp without first paralyzing him.

Hellin: Now hurry your ass back on the train with Orsela while I deal with this fucker.

Kthanid: You don't gotta tell me twice, Princess.

Kthanid hurried away from his attacker and re-entered the train to assist Orsela. With Kthanid no longer a worry, Hellin released the Assailant's mind, and entered into her battle stance.

Tentacle Arm Assailant: ...You witch! How dare you corrupt my mind and force me to free that traitor? Do you have any idea what you just did?

Hellin: Don't know and most certainly don't fucking care. Perhaps if you had waited until after the train reached its destination, I may have minded my damn business while you dealt with Kthanid. However, you decided to interrupt my train ride, so now I end your life!

Setting both her hands ablaze in black colored flames, Hellin rushed to the Tentacle Arm Assailant with a flurry of strikes. The Assailant dodged the inhumanly fast strikes and swiftly swung his tentacle to knock Hellin away. Having blocked the tentacle right before it hit her, Hellin managed to not only reduce whatever damage she may have suffered, but she also managed to keep herself from falling off the moving train.

Tentacle Arm Assailant: Let's see you defend against this, demon...

(((Electric Poison)))

Faster than the speed of lightning, the Tentacle Arm Assailant unleashed a dirty green colored electric current from his tentacle, striking Hellin with perfect precision. Hellin instantly dropped to her knees and her skin became sickly looking.

Tentacle Arm Assailant: Arrogant little wrench! Not feeling so hot now, huh? Don't count on your demon regenerative abilities to heal you from this poisonous attack of mine. In less than thirty seconds, your body will shut down completely. But first, I'm going to cut your damn head off and keep it as a trophy for your defiance!

Slowly walking towards the weakened Hellin, the Tentacle Arm Assailant transformed the tip of his tentacle into the shape of a blade. Standing over the poisoned Hellin, the Assailant raised his tentacle in the air and prepared to decapitate her. Right before he attempted to finish her off, Hellin ran her right arm straight into the Assailant's chest like a bullet. Feeling himself dying, he looked at the demon in sheer horror. With murder in her eyes, Hellin coldly explained to the alien how she easily recovered from his deadly attack.

Hellin: You're probably wondering why your pathetic poison didn't finish me off. Well, the fact of the matter is, I was playing possum. Your attack was indeed fast but unfortunately for you, it was a poison-based attack. Something you must now realize is *useless* against me! Not that it's going to matter once I kill you but my mother, the Queen of Babylon, is a master of poison-based attacks. As part of my training, my mother introduced a variety of poisons to my body and forced me to adapt to each and every single one. The poison in your attack was the weakest I have ever felt enter my body. I almost had a hard time faking the ineffectiveness of your poison in my body. I didn't need to use my telepathy to destroy you, after all. Now, say hello to your maker for me!

Before the Assailant could even think to beg for his life, Hellin ferociously ripped his rib cage out of his chest. She then kicked the dead man off the moving train before tossing his ribs and re-entering the train.

Orsela: Hellin! I knew you would be alright but another minute longer, I would've joined you.

Kthanid: Thank you for saving my life, Princess.

Hellin: Orsela, you know I appreciate you always having my back, but I would have been pissed if you came to aid me against such a small fry. As for you, Kthanid...if you don't get fifty fucking feet away from me once we reach Texas, let's just say Cthulhu will be the least of your fucking worries.

Kthanid: I apologize that one of my assailants had managed to find me and cause so much trouble for everyone on board.

Orsela: Hellin may be pissed, but we know it's not your fault, Kthanid.

Hellin: Speak for yourself, Orsela. He just better be thankful I had something to kill on this otherwise boring ass trip.

Kthanid: Well, Orsela and I were successful in calming down the passengers on board. I even told the conductor that you were an agent of King Onyx and that you had the situation under control and there was no need to call for help or stop the train. We are now less than twenty minutes away from arriving in Texas.

Orsela: Indeed! I'm so excited to see our friend August again.

Hellin: Hmph.

✦

After successfully defeating the Assailant and reaching Texas, the girls bade Kthanid farewell before going their separate ways. The girls headed to a nearby bar that August frequented to relax after a day of fighting off troublesome Sages. They arrived at the bar minutes later and spotted August drinking his usual cranberry whiskey while chilling over at the pool table. August spotted the girls walking towards him and placed his drink on the pool table.

August: Howdy ladies! It's truly good to see y'all again.

Hellin: You better not be drunk already, cowboy. We need you sober for this trip to Nigeria.

August: Trust me, Princess, this cowboy is barely even buzzed. However, if you two arrived a little later, I definitely would've been half-naked and dancing on top of this pool table.

Orsela: Thank goodness we got here when we did then. Considering what happened earlier, we thought we'd end up getting here late.

Hellin: Now that the three of us are together, let's go to this teleporter and get down to business.

August: Oh yeah, let me call Lea now that you two girls are here.

Orsela: Oh, so Lea is our teleporter? Just great.

Hellin: Lea? Not that annoying, self-absorbed bitch! Damn you, Onyx!

4

The Annoying Princess of Plutonia

STARFINDER and Orsela managed to calm down Hellin before she made a further ruckus at the bar. The three of them then made their way to meet up with Lea, Princess of Plutonia, and one of the strongest teleporters to ever exist. Sadly, Lea was an elitist snob, and downright dreadful to be around at times. The worst part is, Hellin and Orsela had come to know just her personality since first meeting her a few years ago. Starfinder, on the other hand, only knew Lea as Princess of one of the most powerful countries in Europe. This would be his first time meeting her in person. He, too, would learn why neither woman is thrilled to see Lea again.

Starfinder: Okay, ladies, we gotta go to the Gold Hotel to meet our lady teleporter. Let me go hitch a ride there because we damn sure ain't walking twenty miles to get there. While I know you demons have inhuman stamina, I ain't no demon and long walks get on my nerves.

Hellin: You're a Bounty Hunter. You should be used to walking a lot. ...Whatever. Just go find us a ride.

Starfinder tipped his hat to the girls before going off in search of a ride. Hellin then turned to Orsela and explained her annoyance with their current situation.

Hellin: Orsela, I'm so fucking pissed! Bad enough Onyx convinced our mother to send us to Nigeria to find a missing boy, who could already be dead for all we know. Now that bastard is having us work with that annoying ass self-centered bitch once again. I swear if it wasn't for our mother, I would've already ripped that man's head off his fucking shoulders.

Orsela: Well, I can't stand being around Lea either, Hellin. We have to remember because of the situation in Nigeria, no one can directly teleport into the country, especially demons. While Onyx could have probably found us a less insufferable teleporter, at least we know Lea and she's very good at what she does. Besides, look at it this way, Hellin...at least it's not Okubi.

Just hearing Okubi's name come out of Orsela's mouth caused Hellin to make a face mixed with disgust and, surprisingly, fear. While Hellin didn't fear any living being, with the exception of her mother, she vividly remembered her confrontation with Okubi several years prior when he nearly killed her. Things between them have become amicable since they battled one another, yet tension between Hellin and Okubi still remained. Like Lea, Okubi was another highly skilled teleporter who would have been equally useful for their current mission. However, between dealing with Lea or Okubi, even Hellin would painfully admit that Lea was the better choice. Realizing this, Hellin took a deep breath before responding to Orsela.

Hellin: You know how much I hate it when you make a good point, Orsela, but yeah...I guess it's better to be dealing with Lea.

Orsela: That's just me being the voice of reason...and it seems Starfinder found us a ride.

Hellin turned in Starfinder's direction. The bounty hunter signaled the girls to follow him. They then entered the wagon procured by Starfinder. Arriving at the luxurious place that is the Gold Hotel, the trio checked in before taking the elevator to the 45th floor. They walked to the suite with Starfinder leading the way. Before his right hand could knock on the door, a voice inside shouted out, "It's open." Hellin used her telepathy to ensure the person inside was Lea and once doing so, telepathically told Starfinder to go inside as they followed. Although Hellin checked to ascertain who was on the other side of the door, not even she knew that upon stepping inside the room that the three of them would lay eyes on a naked buxom woman with soft French vanilla colored skin and long brown hair with caramel streaks past her shoulders. Orsela quickly covered her eyes in shock. Starfinder's face turned red with a slight erection in his pants. Hellin just stared at Lea with annoyance all over her face.

Lea: Hey gang, I sensed that you three were coming, so I left the door unlocked.

Hellin: Lea! Why in the hell are you butt-ass naked?

Lea: This is my suite, Hellin, so I'll do as I please. Besides, my body is a work of art and I have no shame being naked. The cowboy doesn't look like he minds.

Starfinder: Pardon me, Princess, but I couldn't help myself in front of such a beautiful woman.

Starfinder removed his hat and placed it over his crotch.

Hellin: That's because Starfinder is a typical man. Now put some damn clothes on, so you can open up a portal for us to Cameroon.

Orsela: Or, she can just do that now since she doesn't need to be dressed to open a portal.

Lea: About that portal to Cameroon...of course, I promised Onyx that I would help you guys get as close to Nigeria as possible, since Aliyu placed a spell that forbids teleporting directly into Nigeria without consequences. However, I do have one condition before I portal you three to Cameroon...

Hellin: And what is that, Lea?

Lea: Let me join your mission.

Hellin: Abso-fucking-lutely not! Bad enough Starfinder has to tag along, but you are not part of the deal, Stallard.

Lea: Well, either I go or find yourself another teleporter. Not that it would be impossible, but there are very few teleporters strong enough to take someone all the way from Texas to Nigeria; let alone more than one person.

Hellin: Lea, you little bitch! Make that portal for us right now or so help me Satan, I'll take over your mind and force you to create a portal for us before making you kill yourself! Now stop being a fucking diva and open up a portal for us!

Lea: Nope! Besides, do you really want to start a war between Plutonia and Babylon, Princess Hellin?

Hellin: Lea, you fucking—

Orsela: Fine! You can come with us, Lea.

Hellin: Orsela!

Orsela: Hellin, we don't have time for this right now. Trevyn's life is in jeopardy and every second we waste lessens our chances of finding him alive and catching his captors. If it means bringing Lea along on the mission, so be it. I'm positive Onyx won't mind, but that requires you being okay with it.

Lea: So, what's it going to be, Hellin?

Hellin: You little entitled bitch! Dammit! As much as it pains me to say it, Orsela is absolutely right.

Lea: I'll take that as a yes.

Orsela: Yes, you can come, but hurry up and get dressed. We are literally racing against time. And one more thing, Lea.

Lea: What, Orsela?

Orsela: If you do anything stupid to jeopardize the success of our mission, Hellin will be the least of your problems.

Lea: Yeah, yeah, yeah, you can stop behaving like typical demons. I promise to be as useful as humanly possible since that's what I am, after all.

Hellin: If you wanted to be useful, you would jump into a pit of red lions.

Lea: Hellin, you're such a sweetheart. I almost can't stand it.

Lea grabbed a towel off the vanity and went to the bathroom to quickly get dressed. Minutes later Lea reappeared dressed in her signature custom-made white qipao dress with her hair now in an elegant bun. Now with everyone ready, Lea stood before the others as her eyes changed colors. A multi-colored portal opened from behind her. The four then entered the portal and arrived in Cameroon within minutes. They quickly found a Rider within Cameroon, after explaining their situation. The man gladly took them as close to Nigeria as possible. Their journey towards Nigeria started off smoothly. Suddenly, they saw from afar what appeared to be a storm brewing within Nigeria. Hellin, her teammates, and the Rider looked concerned and confused; knowing for a fact that there shouldn't be any bad weather taking place in Nigeria. Using her telepathic powers, Hellin sensed that something unsettling was happening within Nigeria, proving indeed that the storm wasn't a natural occurrence.

Hellin: Something is very wrong in Nigeria. I can't exactly tell what it is, but there's something definitely wrong.

Starfinder: You can say that again, darling. There ain't supposed to be no type of storm happening in Nigeria, especially today.

Rider: Well, unless our eyes and ears are deceiving us, that is definitely a storm happening within Nigeria. I'm sorry to inform you all, but I cannot journey any further towards Nigeria.

Orsela: That's understandable, Mr. François, but *we* cannot turn back.

Hellin: Which means we get off now while you head back to safety in Cameroon.

Lea: And do what, walk?

Starfinder: Darling, I thought you were going to be on your best behavior if we allowed you to tag along.

Lea: I said no such thing and besides, do you really expect us to walk into a storm?

Orsela: You can open a portal back to Texas or better yet, go home, Princess. No one is forcing you to put yourself in danger.

Lea: Fine! I'll walk towards the stupid storm.

Hellin: You fucking fail to realize that Orsela and I are demons. We can run faster than the average Rider, but with you and Starfinder along, we can't do that. Therefore, Orsela and I have to carry you on our backs while we run the rest of the way into Nigeria. Orsela, carry Lea on your back. I'll carry Starfinder. Mr. François thankfully got us pretty close, so ten minutes of running is all we'll need before we're at the entrance of Nigeria. Then we'll figure out what's up with this unexpected storm before meeting with Queen Aliyu.

François bade Hellin and company farewell before taking off with his horse and carriage back to Cameroon. Hellin carried Starfinder and Orsela carried Lea. They hurried towards the direction of the storm in Nigeria. As the four drew closer to their destination, the demons struggled to hold onto their non-demon allies, but managed to resist the heavy winds and press forward. Finally making it inside of Nigeria, the four found themselves facing the source of the storm that terrorized the citizens of Nigeria.

Standing before them was a muscular, elderly man wearing a brown and golden dashiki outfit that exposed his abs, with prayer beads around his neck, arms, and ankles. Staring with his glowing white hot eyes in the direction of Hellin and her comrades, the man said angrily, "I blame your kind for our suffering!"

5

Team Hellin vs Adewale

THEY KNEW before entering Nigeria that the storm ravaging the country was not natural but created. None of them expected it to be the work of a human Sage. Many Nigerian citizens ran to safety. The damage caused by this man was a catastrophe nonetheless. Barely able to withstand the strong winds, Hellin and her friends stood before the wind-manipulating Sage. Even without reading the man's mind, Hellin could feel his malice towards her and Orsela because they were demons. Knowing that neither Orsela nor she had done anything to this man or even laid eyes on him until now, after hearing the man's angry words, it didn't take a neurosurgeon to realize that the man's vexation was demon-related.

Using her telepathy to swiftly read his mind, Hellin learned that his name was

Adewale, and he was one of Queen Aliyu's Royal Guards of Nigeria. He lashed out because of his beliefs that his Queen's restrictions and the disappearance of her son was caused by the actions of demons. Adewale's resentment towards demons and their eligibility to inhabit Nigeria made his heart turn sour towards both his Queen and his people. Adewale decided that Nigeria will be free of the inhabitants of evil one way or another. Thus, he created a massive storm to devastate his homeland. Although Hellin had successfully obtained this information from the enraged Sage, Adewale had detected Hellin roaming within his mind.

Adewale: So not only are you a filthy demon, but you *dare* invade my thoughts as though they are yours!

Before anyone had time to react, Adewale unleashed a powerful stream of wind at Hellin, sending her crashing to the ground. Orsela, angered at witnessing her sister-friend being attacked, attempted to summon one of her Nox monsters to fight Adewale. Before she was able to do so, Adewale struck Orsela with a blast of wind that sent her crashing to the ground as well. Starfinder and Lea momentarily stared at the terror before the anger inside Starfinder kicked in and he drew his guns towards Adewale.

Adewale: I could have struck all four of you if I wished, but I sensed the two of you are not demons. Even though it disgusts me to see humans in the company of demons, if you turn away now, I will spare your lives. Otherwise, you, too, will suffer my wrath.

Starfinder: Fuck you, asshole! Those are my friends you just attacked.

Starfinder immediately started firing powerful energy bullets from his gun as Adewale created a shield of wind to defend against the barrage of bullets. Lea quickly placed her right hand between her breast and pulled out an explosive bead before throwing it in Adewale's direction. The explosion managed to break Adewale's shield. The force pushed him back, but he remained on his feet. Angered by the resistance of Starfinder and Lea, the Sage unleashed a burst of wind. Starfinder and Lea flew up in the air before dropping to the ground. Before Adewale could make his next move, Orsela charged towards him and released a flurry of powerful kicks. Using his wind-based magic, Adewale generated a shield of wind on his fist to defend against the demon's flurry of deadly kicks.

Orsela: I don't know what your fucking problem is, but I'm going to kick your ass for attacking my friends.

Adewale: I gave your friends a chance to flee, but they chose to fight like fools instead. I only did enough damage to knock them out, but they should survive. However, I have no intention of holding back against a disgusting demon like you!

Orsela continued a merciless offense against Adewale, but the Sage was able to block each and every one of her deadly strikes. Spotting an opening, Adewale swiftly hit Orsela's abdomen with multiple wind-infused palm wallops followed by a ferocious kick to her face, sending her crashing to the ground once again. Adewale's attack was not enough to keep Orsela down, as she continued fighting. However, she sensed the presence of an infuriated Hellin rushing towards Adewale, which caused her to pause. Unable to sense Hellin coming in time, Adewale was caught by Hellin's hands around his neck. She mercilessly slammed the Sage on the ground, rupturing his spine. Adewale screamed out in agony. With her hands still around his neck, she spoke to the seemingly defeated Adewale.

Hellin: Be thankful that I only broke your spine, asshole! How dare you cause such chaos knowing the situation that's happening within your country. Furthermore, how fucking dare you attack my friends and me!

Adewale: You should've killed me, demon, and now I'm going to make you regret it.

Suddenly, a burst of energy emanated from Adewale, knocking Hellin off of him. Absorbing the massive energy of his storm, the Sage not only repaired his broken spine, but Adewale's brown skin changed colors. The winds became more ferocious as a grayish-red aura surrounded Adewale's body. His skin turned from its natural color to mahogany. The prayer beads that were once perfectly placed on his body now floated sporadically around his neck, arms, and ankles. Now transformed, Adewale stared murderously at the woman demons. Sensing how strong he'd become, Hellin sent a telepathic message to Orsela to check on Starfinder and Lea. Hellin knew she must take out Adewale once and for all. Orsela hesitated at first but Hellin gave her a commanding glare, forcing Orsela to leave her friend to fend for herself.

Transformed Adewale: Filthy demons! I knew nothing good could ever come from allowing your kind into our country. That fool, Aliyu, became too familiar with that demon King of Mayland. He influenced her to allow such vermin into our sacred land. Now

I must destroy it in order to save it. I also blame your kind for the death of Prince Trevyn.

Hellin: Fuck you, asshole! Prince Trevyn is only missing, not dead! I don't give two fucks about what you think of demons. I personally hate your kind as well, but I'm not egotistical enough to allow my beliefs to dictate how everyone else should think. If Queen Aliyu doesn't mind demons on her lands, who the fuck are you to say otherwise?

Transformed Adewale: I care *not* for your words, demon! Queen Aliyu turned her back on her people the day she allowed your kind to infest our land. She *betrayed* us first! I'm done talking to you. Now with my full powers, I shall finish you off for good! Then I'll get rid of your friends before saving my homeland.

Hellin: Every minute I waste here with you, motherfucker, is time wasted finding Trevyn. If I don't accomplish anything else today, I'm going to make you fucking regret ever crossing paths with me.

Transformed Adewale: Time to die!

Adewale whipped up two large spirals of grayish-red winds and hurled them at Hellin.

Using her demonic super-speed, she easily avoided the attacks as she ran towards the Sage. Refusing to give up, he then launched several blades of wind towards his target. Dodging most of the blades of winds with only one managing to strike her arm, Hellin shrugged the cut off as the wound rapidly healed, and moved towards her opponent. Once in striking range, she unleashed a flood of deadly punches and kicks against Adewale. Using the same method he previously used against Orsela, the Sage created a shield of wind to defend against the demon's strike. Unlike Orsela, Hellin proved too much for him as she successfully broke through his shield and delivered a fearsome punch to his gut, sending the Sage crashing to the ground. Wasting no time, Hellin followed up with her attack (((*Beautiful Tragedy*))), and lobbed a cyan, magenta, and yellow giant ball of fire towards Adewale. Rising to his feet in the nick of time, Adewale manipulated a wind barrier to neutralize the demon's fiery attack.

Realizing that Hellin is stronger than any foe he has ever faced, Adewale prepared to use his ultimate Forbidden Technique. "You have proven yourself too much of a nuisance, demon!" The Sage held his arms out wide as he began forming deadly grayish-red spirals of winds all around him. Hellin, sensing that the Sage was preparing a devastating attack, decided not to strike him or use her telepathy to stop him in his tracks. Instead, she summoned a powerful reddish-black aura around her body; an ability she called ((((*Satanic Veil*)))). It allowed Hellin to absorb a fatal blow while only receiving a tenth of the damage that her opponent's attack could cause. She knew that such an attack would exhaust Adewale, and she could then finish him off with ease.

However, right before Adewale could complete his onslaught against her, out of nowhere, a golden needle flew towards Adewale. It struck his neck and caused him to transform back to his normal self instantly as he crumbled to the ground. Hellin immediately turned in the direction of the pin and spotted Queen Aliyu herself, dressed in her typical regal Nigerian garb, alongside two of her bodyguards. One was a tall albino man wearing a green and silver dashiki with a spear in his hand and the other was an anthropomorphic civet muscular man. Looking at the destruction all around her caused by her once-loyal servant Adewale, Queen Aliyu fought the urge to summon her amethyst blade to behead the unconscious Sage. Unaware that the battle had already ended, Orsela along with Lea and a fully recovered Starfinder rushed to aid Hellin. They saw Adewale unconscious on the ground, and the unexpected presence of Nigeria's current ruler with her two guards.

Starfinder: I guess the party's over, huh?

Hellin: Obviously! What the hell did you do to him, Aliyu?

Queen Aliyu: That's *Queen* Aliyu to you, Princess of Babylon. I simply struck the traitorous Adewale with one of my golden needles to a pressure point in his neck while he was distracted trying to unleash a deadly attack against you. Speaking of which, why didn't you just use your telepathy to shut his mind down? Didn't he cause enough damage to my country? Why insist upon a fist fight when you can manipulate your opponent's mind?

Hellin: I'll use my powers as I damn well please. Unlike my mother and Onyx, I don't rely on my telepathy to solve my problems.

Queen Aliyu: How short-sighted of you. Rashawn, Vicet, one of you, get that traitor off the ground and bring him back to my castle. Hellin and company, follow us to my castle. We have much to discuss.

Lea: So, what about all this damage caused by that mad man of yours?

Queen Aliyu: Worry not, Princess Stallard. I already have a team of skilled Sages repairing various areas affected by the storm created by that fool Adewale. Now cease saying anything further until we reach the castle or I'll have you thrown in prison for being annoying.

Lea huffed. Before she could be her typical exasperating self, Hellin gave her a cold stare and the Princess of Plutonia reluctantly behaved herself as the group headed to Queen Aliyu's castle.

Meanwhile, hidden in a laboratory in an undisclosed location in Eket, Nigeria, Dr. Ezekiel and his cohorts had seen with their spy cams placed throughout Nigeria, minus the Queen's Castle, not only the cause of the storm but the battle between Hellin's group and the traitorous Adewale. The storm itself was no threat to Dr. Ezekiel's plans. The fact that Hellin, a known associate of King Onyx, along with bounty hunter August Starfinder, Princess Lea Stallard, and the yellow and green haired woman were in Nigeria troubled him. Sensing that something was wrong with their boss, the Miles Brothers stopped what they were doing and checked on him.

Alec: Hey, Ezekiel, is everything all right?

Richard: Glad the storm finally stopped. The noise made it difficult to concentrate. So, what's on your mind, boss?

Dr. Ezekiel: It's probably nothing to concern ourselves with but just in case, how is the test subject coming along?

Richard: Prince Aliyu has proven to be the best test subject for *Project Demon Slayer*. His transformation is nearly complete.

Alec: Once we know how to perfect an artificial angel, we can then seek other candidates and turn them into artificial angels as well. Once we have enough of them, we can carry out our ultimate ambitions.

Richard: Which is to rid this world of all demons.

Dr. Ezekiel: That's good to hear. I couldn't ask for better men to work on this project with me than the two of you. While we have no need to fear our location ever being discovered thanks to the anti-detector spells we carefully placed in our vicinity, I do have some concerns about that Hellin woman and her company being in Nigeria. In case they do prove to be a kink in our plans, we may need to speed up the process of the test subject's transformation.

Richard: I don't think that filthy demon and her allies will be any threat to us; especially once our project is finished. The power of an artificial angel is enough to rid any demon. So, should they be unfortunate enough to find us...

Alec: They will meet their demise by our ultimate weapon.

Dr. Ezekiel: Music to my ears, gentlemen. Now let us not waste any more time and conclude this project. The sooner we begin the eradication of demons, the better this world shall be...along with all those who worship those abominations.

6

Forbidden Technique: Omnipresent Sight!

SHORTLY after arriving at Queen Aliyu's castle, the heroes were escorted by the Queen's servant, Louise, to the guest area to relax. Meanwhile, Rashawn and Vicet threw Adewale into a cell within the castle's dungeons and placed an anti-magic collar on his neck because of his earlier actions. Sitting in the guest area, the heroes talked amongst themselves, and planned their next move.

Hellin: So, I wonder how long Queen Aliyu is going to have us hang around her castle? Adewale has been dealt with, so us sitting here is just a waste of time.

Lea: Maybe she has some information she wants to share with us regarding her son's disappearance?

Starfinder: I strongly doubt that's the case, ladies. If Queen Aliyu had any leads to her son's whereabouts, trust and believe, the four of us wouldn't be here right about now.

Orsela: I'm afraid you may actually be right, Starfinder. Then what possible reason would Queen Aliyu ask us to wait here until she returns?

Hellin: She mentioned before we reached her castle that she was going to contact Onyx. I guess she's going to update us first on her conversation with Onyx before sending us off to find Trevyn.

Starfinder: Let's hope that's the case, darling, but I fear the news she'll have for us is not of the good variety.

Hellin: And people say I'm pessimistic.

Moments later, Miss Louise returned to the heroes, but asked only Hellin to come with her while the rest remained in the guest area. Hellin followed Louise to Queen Aliyu's throne. Sitting before the Queen was, of course, Rashawn and Vicet.

Queen Aliyu: I didn't say this earlier due to the chaos caused by that fool Adewale. However, I wanted to thank you and the others for journeying all this way to my country. I know it wasn't easy because of all the restrictions I have in place, but that's only because I want to find my son.

Hellin: It's fine, Aliyu. As for Trevyn, any word on where he could possibly be?

Queen Aliyu: About my son, Hellin ...that's why I brought you here alone to speak on the matter. As much as it pains me, since Trevyn is my pride and joy, nothing in this world matters more to me than him...except Nigeria herself...

Hellin: Wait...what are you saying?

Queen Aliyu: It pains me, Hellin, but I think it's best for you and your team to return to Mayland. As you know, my son's friends' bodies were already found floating in the Imo River. I'm pretty sure my son has already met a similar fate. Besides, ever since my lockdown of Nigeria, it has caused my citizens, both humans and demons, great unrest. I love Trevyn so much, but I cannot allow my entire country to suffer over one individual. Even if that one individual is my own child.

Hellin: Are you mad? My friends and I didn't go through all of this just to turn back. Just give us a chance, Aliyu. We will search every fucking part of Nigeria until we find the bastards who had the audacity to kidnap Trevyn and murder his friends. I mean, what would Onyx think about this? He wouldn't just give up on Trevyn, and you shouldn't either.

Queen Aliyu: As noble as your cause is, Hellin, I cannot subject my people to such suffering. I'm practically holding all Nigerians hostage for the actions of people who probably aren't even from this land. I want Trevyn back so bad, but I have a responsibility to my people as well. If I don't act soon, Adewale won't be the only revolt this country shall face. If I lose favor with my citizens then I have failed as Nigeria's Queen.

Hellin: Fuck that! Trevyn is your son and should be a greater priority than any of these fuckers here. My friends and I came this far and now you just want us to go back home like nothing happened? No disrespect, but I cannot accept that, Aliyu. Even if I have to find Trevyn, dead or alive, without your blessing, I will do just that and I *dare* anyone to try and stop me!

Queen Aliyu: You know, Princess Strongs, if you were to speak to me like this under different circumstances, I would've already ordered my guards to kill you...even knowing that you probably could slay most of them on your own. However, I know you truly want to find Trevyn or at the very least, make my son's captors suffer for their crimes. The problem is, Hellin, I sent my best people to search everywhere within this country and not a soul has been able to find a remote lead on where Trevyn could be. Even using spells to find someone who's lost has led to empty results.

Hellin: Well, that's more reason you need to let my friends and me search this bitch! Just because these asswipes managed to evade your men doesn't mean they are going to be as lucky dealing with my team and me.

Queen Aliyu: As much as you may not want to hear this, Hellin, you truly are the yang to Onyx's yin. He pretty much had the same conviction in finding Trevyn over the conversation we had on the phone. He strongly disagrees with me giving up the search for my son. I told him let me see if you felt the same way first. Otherwise, no matter how he felt, I would have removed my anti-teleportation spell off Nigeria, and allowed Princess Stallard to open a portal to take the four of you home. Since you are just as passionate as he is about finding Trevyn, I will now instruct Louise to take you to my office, so that you may speak to Onyx in private.

Hellin: Wait...Onyx is on the phone?

Queen Aliyu: He is indeed on the phone. I didn't even hang it up since I knew he wanted to speak to you afterwards. Since you decided against returning to Mayland, the phone is the only way the two of you can converse. Now, Louise, please take Princess Strongs to my office and make sure to leave her alone once she's inside.

Without saying another word to Queen Aliyu, Hellin turned her attention to Louise and followed her to the Queen's office. Once inside she spotted an ivory phone off its base and picked it up immediately.

Hellin: Onyx?

Onyx: Hellin!

Hellin: Look, asshole, I don't have time for bullshit! What is it you wish to speak to me about?

Onyx: Okay, okay, Hellin, just trying to have some fun.

Hellin: Fun with you? Pass! Now just get to the damn point of this conversation.

Onyx: Alrighty then. Well, as I can tell since you're speaking on the phone with me instead of in person at my castle, you did the noble thing and decided to remain in Nigeria until Trevyn is found dead or alive. Of course, we're crossing fingers he's alive. However, we have one problem…

Hellin: That problem being?

Onyx: We have no concrete lead as to where Trevyn is being held hostage in his homeland.

Hellin: I'll tell you just like I told Aliyu. I will search this bitch piece-by-piece until I find the bastards who took Trevyn! So, if that's what you wanted to talk to me about, you can shove that phone you're holding right up your ass.

Onyx: I probably could, Hellin, but I have actual toys for that, thank you very much.

Hellin: Gross!

Onyx: Anyways, while that's one way to go about finding Trevyn, by searching Nigeria "piece-by-piece". Whatever the fuck that means. I, my dear, have a much more effective way for us to locate Trevyn, and it's foolproof at that.

Hellin: So, if you have a solid way to find Trevyn…why the fuck didn't you say something sooner! Let alone tell Queen Aliyu, because she has all but given up hope of ever seeing her son alive again.

Onyx: I didn't tell her because my words alone aren't going to comfort a woman who was just crying on the phone with me before she composed herself to talk to you.

Hellin: Aliyu was crying on the phone with you? I knew I sensed her sadness. I thought I just had an overactive imagination, considering she didn't seem sad when we just spoke.

Onyx: Perhaps you should rely more on your telepathic powers, which include empathetic abilities to sense what someone is truly feeling even if their face doesn't show it. Fortunately, now that you're in Nigeria, the two of us can combine our psychic powers, which my spell requires, and finally find where Trevyn is being kept.

Hellin: A tracking spell? Didn't Aliyu tell you that she and her people already tried that, but nothing worked?

Onyx: Well, of course she did, dumb dumb, but what you and I are about to do goes way beyond the typical tracking spell. We'll be using a Forbidden Technique to find Trevyn.

Hellin gasped upon hearing Onyx mention a Forbidden Technique.

Onyx: There's no need to fear, Hellin... at least on your end. I'm going to handle the ramifications of the effects of using a Forbidden Technique. I just need you to be in sync with me in order for me to use the Forbidden Technique known as (((*Omnipresent Sight*))).

Hellin: And what is this technique going to do?

Onyx: If you know the definition of the word: Omnipresent, it shouldn't be all that hard to figure out, but I shall tell you anyways. Using (((*Omnipresent Sight*))) allows us to find anyone or anything that's missing, no matter where it is in the world. Even if it's a person who's already dead, as long as the corpse itself remains. Now, Hellin, please calm your mind and think of your favorite color.

Hellin: My favorite what?

Onyx: Hellin, please follow my damn instructions!

Hellin: Fine, asshole!

Calming her mind, she thought of a color she liked. While not the type to have a favorite color; *What kind of childish ass has a favorite color?* Hellin decided on the color red because it was the color of her mission outfit. On the other side of the world in his castle, King Onyx did the same. Focusing on his favorite color, creamy pink, a few minutes passed before both Hellin and Onyx fell into a trance. Seconds later they found themselves in a place known as the Astral Plane; a place only psychics are able to visit when at a high level of mental concentration. Both of them appeared in the unique realm as ghost-like beings; Hellin was red and Onyx was creamy pink. Holding each other's hands, they created a psychic projection of the events that took place the night of Trevyn's kidnapping; seeing events play out as if they were their own.

Hellin and Onyx saw Trevyn and his friends playing in the park before two men in lab coats threw knockout gas on the playground and put them to sleep. They then took them to a laboratory hidden deep near the Shebshi Mountains. Hellin and Onyx then saw a vision of Trevyn being tortured by the men in white lab coats before seeing him slowly being transformed into something not human. They received a last vision of Trevyn with glowing white eyes before Onyx began fading away as the Astral Plane went dark on them. Hellin, unable to process everything happening in the Astral Plane now, knew for certain that Trevyn was still alive and exactly where he was being kept. Before she could realize what happened, Hellin awakened back into her body. Immediately, she went to the phone and called out Onyx's name to no avail. Yura picked up the phone on the other end.

Hellin: Yura, where's Onyx?

Yura: Did you find the boy's location?

Hellin: Yes, bitch, but that doesn't answer my question. Where is Onyx? He disappeared before the Astral Plane thingy kicked me out.

Yura: The King of Mayland is not your concern. Do as you were told and finish your mission.

Yura hung up before Hellin could get in another word. Although angry and uncommonly worried about what was going on with Onyx, she ultimately decided to focus on the task at hand.

Meanwhile in his castle, Onyx suffered the ramifications of using the Forbidden Spell. He fell into a psychic coma and collapsed in Yura's arms. She held onto her boss and friend as she prayed he wasn't mistaken in utilizing such powerful techniques, and would soon wake up.

Hellin returned to Queen Aliyu with a look of determination. She asked Miss Louise to bring her friends to the throne quarters because she had something imperative to announce to all of them. Miss Louise departed briefly to oblige Hellin's request. Once her team arrived, Hellin spoke passionately to all of them.

Hellin: Listen up, motherfuckers! Thanks to Onyx and me putting our heads together, in more ways than one, I now know exactly where Trevyn is being held. Not only are we going to rescue him, but we're gonna make the bastards who kidnapped him pay!

7

Along Came a Deceiver

THEY MADE a hasty exit from Queen Aliyu's castle, and journeyed to the Shebshi Mountains. Hellin and the others couldn't help but sense someone was following them. Whatever was following them was immune to being scented out by the demons as well as Hellin's telepathy. While the thought of an unknown being tracking them was far from comforting, Hellin knew the moment that individual made a move that she would show no mercy and rip it apart limb for limb.

Meanwhile, finding Trevyn was her number one priority although subconsciously, she worried about what happened to Onyx after their ordeal in the Astral Plane. That wasn't important now because the bitch, Yura, said she needed to focus only on her mission. Moving closer to the Shebshi Mountains, Hellin and the others noticed defective spy cameras lying on the ground and hanging from trees as they drew closer to the hideout. Sensing something was off, August signaled for the girls to take a moment before approaching.

August: I know I ain't the one calling the shots here, but we need to call out this fucking weirdness with all these damn cameras.

Lea: It is rather unsettling since we've been spotting them ever since we got closer to the mountains.

Orsela: Not to mention that something or someone is following us, yet we can't tell what it is exactly.

Hellin: The cameras are fucking weird, but the fact that they're defective is even more concerning. Obviously, Trevyn's kidnappers set them up to keep an eye on things in Nigeria. But, the one deactivating them is who we should be concerned with at the moment. Speaking of which...get from behind that fucking boulder or else!

A vanilla-skinned woman wearing her strawberry blonde hair with pink, lime green, and sky blue streaks slicked into a ponytail stepped from behind the boulder that was only a few feet from where Hellin and her team stood. She donned her signature skintight catsuit. While Lea had no clue who this woman was, Hellin, Orsela, and Starfinder all said in unison, with a mixture of terror and anger in their voices, "Love!"

Love: I should've known this damn talisman wasn't going to keep me hidden from you forever, Helly Welly! That's what I get for just snagging one of these off a witch in Louisiana. Oh hello, Orsellie Momellie and August Longdick. It's been a while.

Starfinder: So, it was you following us all the way here.

Orsela: What's your business here, assassin? You better not be working with Trevyn's kidnappers.

Hellin: Oh, she better not be...for her fucking sake.

Lea: Who in the hell is this chick?

Love: Girl, who the hell are you?

Lea: What? I'm Lea Stallard, the Princess of Plutonia.

Love: Never heard of you. Sorry, not sorry.

Hellin: Lea, don't say another damn word. Love, what in the hell are you doing here? Better yet, who are you here to kill?

Love: Actually, I'm hoping I don't need to kill anyone this time around. I was hired to rescue Trevyn. Believe it or not.

Hellin: I don't, and I don't need my telepathy to confirm that, murderess.

Love: Oh, not you calling me out for being a killer, when you have done worse under orders of that slutty mother of yours.

Hellin: You watch your damn mouth about my mother!

Love: Okay, that was in bad taste. Please don't kill me, Helly.

Hellin: Stop calling me that name, you broken bitch! Now, for the last time, tell me your *real* purpose for being here before I do what I should've done a long time ago...burn you to a fucking crisp!

Love: I'm not lying. I was hired by a benefactor who wants Prince Trevyn brought back home alive. Obviously, my benefactor isn't Queen Aliyu, but please believe what I am telling you. I'm not here to bring any harm to Prince Trevyn. His survival means the world to me at the moment. Hell, to be fucking frank, if I fail to save Trevyn, I might as well kill myself.

Orsela: Why is saving Trevyn such an obligation for you? Assassins are killers, not heroes.

Love: The person who hired me, Orselie, told me in the bluntest way one can make a request, and I quote, "Bring Trevyn back to his mother alive or I will have you killed for your failure." My benefactor even went as far as to give me all the resources I needed to reach Nigeria.

Hellin: So, you even know about that, but how?

Love: Helly...I mean, Hellin, you do know I'm an assassin or a *murderess* as you so eloquently stated earlier. Therefore, I work with people who are well aware of what's going on in this world...even in yours. I'm also responsible for deactivating the spy cameras that you all saw on the way here. If I hadn't done that, Trevyn's kidnappers would've seen you coming, and that would not have been good. We must surprise those bastards if we want to succeed in rescuing Trevyn.

Starfinder: You seem to know a lot about Trevyn's kidnappers, killer.

Love: I do...just not enough to know what they are capable of. That's why I moved carefully since I arrived in Nigeria...until now.

Hellin: Well, if you weren't being a fucking creep, I wouldn't have called you out so brazenly.

Love: No harm done, Hellin. I was just worried if you guys spotted me before I was ready to be discovered, it would have been quite a misunderstanding; however, if any of you still doubt me—

Lea: I do!

Hellin: Zip it!

Love: My mind is open for you to search, Princess of Babylon.

Hellin: I don't know if it's because I worked alongside you before, assassin, or the fact that I can easily kill you if you dare try to cross us, but I don't sense any intent from you to harm Trevyn. Matter of fact, you seem just as concerned in finding him as my teammates and me.

Love: I just "heart" the fact we are now on the same page. Let's not waste any more time here. Let's go rescue Trevyn. We're almost at the Shebshi Mountains. The base where he's being kept is definitely within that area.

Starfinder: I just got one more question before we shake a leg. Love, did you know that this is where Trevyn was being kept all this time?

Love: Not at all, Longdick! Ever since the four of you arrived in Nigeria, I have been following you in the shadows; since searching for Trevyn alone was ineffective.

Hellin: So, it was you I sensed when we were fighting Adewale.

Love: That would be correct. I must ask why didn't you just take over that crazy Sage's mind and make him kill himself? I swear, Hellin, you're the only telepath I know who hates using her telepathic powers.

Hellin: Playing mind games on people is cheap! Why use my telepathy when my fist does the job just fine? Anyway, enough standing around. We have a Prince to rescue. Love, you're coming with us, if that wasn't already obvious.

Love: Hooray!

Lea: Shit!

With Love now added to their team, the heroes hurried to the Shebshi Mountains to rescue Trevyn. Meanwhile back at their base, the scientists argued amongst themselves and struggled to figure out who deactivated their cameras from the outside. Not being able to carefully watch what's going on in Nigeria, delayed their efforts to complete *Project Demon Slayer.* Richard and Alec worried that someone may have discovered their location. Dr. Nathaniel Ezekiel, so focused on his project being nearly completed, told his two scientists to quell their worries and that they could deploy more cameras outdoors later. Believing that as long as their anti-tracking spells were still in place, even with their cameras destroyed, they would still be hidden until they were ready to reveal themselves. Unfortunately, Dr. Ezekiel was about to find out that all his efforts have been for naught now that Hellin and her crew knew where they were hidden. All their schemes were about to come to a disastrous end.

Finally reaching the mountain, Love pulled out a device that detected any form of machinery hidden in the area even if it's being magically cloaked. The device started beeping as it located the base concealed in the depths of the underground. Hellin readied herself to deliver a powerful punch to the ground that would break a hole deep enough for them to fall into the base. However, Love held her hand out to prevent Hellin from punching the ground.

Hellin: Love, why are you in my fucking way? Didn't I tell you earlier not to be a nuisance?

Love: Not trying to be one either, dear, but I feel what you are about to do is unnecessary, considering that you have a teleporter in the group.

Lea: ... Wait, how did you know I'm a teleporter? You little *bitch*, you know exactly who I am.

Love: Unfortunately, and the rumors about your arrogance were painfully not exaggerated, Princess Stallard.

Orsela: Well, that's great you know who Lea is, but do you also know that Queen Aliyu's anti-teleportation spell is still in effect?

Love: Oh, I do, darling, but since the base where Trevyn is being held is under the protection of anti-tracking spells, technically, it's not part of Nigeria, so we can teleport inside of it. However, it does require one more thing for that plan to work.

Starfinder: Let me guess...Hellin's telepathy?

Love: Good boy! Yes, all we need is Hellin to read one of the mind's inside of the underground laboratory. Then she can broadcast the location into Stallard's mind, and she can teleport us all inside.

Hellin: Then let's not waste any more fucking time. Thank you for being useful for once, Love.

Love: My pleasure, Miss Legend in the Making.

Ignoring Love's comment, Hellin used her telepathy to read the minds of the scientists inside. Entering Alec's head, who was unable to detect a telepath's presence in his mind, Hellin saw everything from the base setup to his twin brother, Richard, and lastly, the man behind it all, Dr. Nathaniel Ezekiel. She then shot a telepathic vision into Lea's head to show her the base as well. Now with both women having seen the inside of the base, Lea activated her powers once again and created a portal for them to enter inside the underground laboratory. Less than two seconds later, the three scientists found themselves face-to-face with Hellin and her crew.

Dr. Alec Miles: What in the fuck?

Dr. Richard Miles: I knew it! Once the cameras were deactivated, it was only a matter of time before we were found. Nathaniel, you goddamn fool!

Dr. Ezekiel: No! How could this be? We did everything right, but we were still discovered!

Hellin: So, you're the fucking bastards who kidnapped Trevyn! I'm going to enjoy every fucking minute of beating the living shit out of each and every one of you motherfuckers!

Love: Nathaniel, it's been a minute, sweetie!

Dr. Ezekiel: Assassin! Oh no, if you're here that means *he* knows what I did and sent you to kill me.

Hellin: Love...I thought you were here to rescue Trevyn?

Love: See, that's why you should use your telepathy, dearie. I couldn't give a flying fuck about Trevyn. I only came here to kill that bastard right there.

Love pulled out a butterfly knife and pointed it directly at Ezekiel. Horrified by the sight of the assassin, Ezekiel ran deeper into the laboratory. Love blew a kiss at a furious Hellin and the others before chasing down her target. The Miles twins now remained faced with Hellin and the other heroes.

Alec: Shit, Brother, I hate that we're in such a predicament!

Richard: The money was good, but I knew all of this was going to catch up to us. Dammit, we don't stand a chance against these demons.

Lea: Hey, only those two girls there are demons. The cowboy and I are one hundred percent human. Still, you assholes are going to pay for kidnapping Trevyn and killing his friends.

Orsela: Speaking of which, Hellin we can deal with these fuckers. Go search this place and find Trevyn. Afterwards, deal with that *bitch!*

Hellin: Thank you, Orsela. Lea! Star-finder! Both of you follow Orsela's lead.

Hellin ran off to search the laboratory to find Trevyn. Both Miles twins realized they were in a bad situation standing against Orsela, Lea, and Starfinder. They decided it was time to pull out their trump card. Reaching inside their lab coat pockets, the twin scientists injected themselves with a needle filled with turquoise-colored liquid. Within seconds, Alec and Richard transformed into two extremely muscular hulk-sized men. Orsela, Starfinder, and Lea readied themselves to battle against the mutated brothers.

8

Demon vs Artificial Angel

WHILE Orsela, Lea, and Starfinder dealt with the mutated Miles brothers, Hellin immediately entered deeper into the underground laboratory to find Trevyn and afterwards, handle that two-timing bitch, Love. After passing several rooms, Hellin sensed a terrible presence...an angelic aura. Normally, an angelic aura would be considered a blessing but for a demon like Hellin, it meant trouble. Not because she feared angels, but because angels possessed powers that most demons cannot handle. By their very nature, an angel's powers are fatal to demons.

Hellin had only met the imperfect angel, Nikiema, who, despite being an angel, was left with her human morality by the King of the Heavens. Outside of her association with Nikiema, Hellin never felt an angelic presence until now. Although tempted to use her telepathy, she decided against it because the angelic aura was strong enough on its own to follow without using her mental powers.

Hellin passed a few more doors before entering a big blue room. Upon stepping inside the room, Hellin was shocked by who stood across from her. It was Trevyn, the son of Queen Aliyu, and the very reason she and her friends traveled to Nigeria in the first place. However, it wasn't Trevyn himself who surprised her. What startled her was the fact that he was the source of the angelic aura she'd sensed. Not only did Trevyn have an angelic aura, but his eyes glowed in a whitish-yellow color and several yellow circles, similar to halos, illuminated around his chest and legs. Though cautious, Hellin realized that just staring at him was going nowhere and thus began to speak.

Hellin: Hey, Trevyn, it's me, Hellin! Your mother sent my comrades and me to find you. Hey! Are you fucking ignoring me, kid?

Irritated but aware that something was off about Trevyn, Hellin now decided to use her telepathy. Reading his mind, Hellin saw more of the horror he'd endured than she did when she and Onyx were in the Astral Plane. Realizing what Dr. Ezekiel and his partners had done to Trevyn, Hellin was overtaken with dread knowing that Trevyn was forcefully transformed into what is called an Artificial Angel; thanks to a Forbidden Technique that Dr. Ezekiel and his partners performed on him in order to create a mortal man with the powers of an angel to exterminate demons like herself. Shortly after reading Trevyn's mind, she felt a murderous intent emanating from him.

Trevyn: Demon! I have been created to eradicate your kind! I shall start with your elimination first!

Hearing Trevyn speak in such a divine but cold voice enraged her, but she knew Trevyn wasn't truly responsible for his actions. Nevertheless, Hellin was not the type to allow someone to harm her; even if they were under the control of someone else. Had this been anyone else, Hellin would have simply killed him. Because it was Trevyn, she didn't have that option. Not only did she not want the blood of the Prince on her hands, but Hellin knew if she killed him, even in self-defense, she would've failed her mission. Both Queen Aliyu and Onyx would come after her. She wasn't afraid of either of them, but having those two as enemies would not be favorable to her or Babylon.

Hellin, therefore, knew she'd have to hold back to not risk killing the young man she was there to save. At the same time, because Trevyn now possessed angelic powers, she had to be careful because a good hit from Trevyn could prove fatal. Hellin knew the strike from an angel neutralized a demon's ability to self-regenerate from fatal wounds. Knowing what she had to do, Hellin stood ready to fight the Prince of Nigeria.

Trevyn created two daggers of light, one in each hand. Without warning, he rushed towards Hellin with the intent to kill her. He swung his holy daggers and tried to decapitate his target. Hellin was able to easily dodge his attacks before delivering a kick to his abdomen, sending him crashing to the ground. Shrugging off the attack, Trevyn increased the size of his angelic daggers and charged at Hellin again. Anger got the better of Hellin, despite knowing she needed to hold back when fighting Trevyn. She again eluded Trevyn's attacks and countered with a powerful blackish-gray blast of fire. Trevyn collapsed after being struck by Hellin's fiery attack. This time he stayed down as the flames engulfed his body. Fearing that she may have seriously injured him, Hellin rushed over to Trevyn. She knelt beside him and patted away flames on various parts of his body.

Unaware of the horror the artificial angel had in store for her, Hellin used her telepathy to scan Trevyn's mind to see if any semblance of his normal self could be reached. Before Hellin could realize it in time, Trevyn used his angelic powers and self-healed right before sticking both his daggers inside Hellin. Shocked by the sudden attack, Hellin wasn't able to even whimper before Trevyn separated the blades within her body, cutting her in half. Hellin lay on the ground, sliced in half, as her intestines hung from her upper body and her own blood pooled around her. Trevyn rose from the ground and watched as Hellin began slowly dying before him.

Feeling herself slip away, all Hellin could think of was how she failed her mother, Orsela, Queen Aliyu, Trevyn, Onyx, and worst of all, herself. Hellin had experienced many near death situations, but always had the luxury of either her (((*Satanic Veil*))) or her self-regenerative abilities to save her. Being fatally wounded by an angel took away all those abilities that would have usually repaired her. Now she lay before the young man she was supposed to save as she started to fade away. Upon closing her eyes, instead of drifting to the Spirit Realm, a place where all souls of the deceased end up, be they mortal or demon, go after death, Hellin found herself once again in the Astral Plane. Rather, she found her half-dead self now lying before her astral self, which she'd created with Onyx only a few hours earlier.

Astral Hellin: This is absolutely fucking ridiculous. If you really think I'm going to allow us to die here, you got another thing coming, bitch! Oh, don't bother speaking, bitch, just save your breath. Lucky for your Mary Sue motherfucking ass, this is not your end! Because of the powers you possess, both physically and mentally, you have unlocked a very special ability known as the (((*Astral Hospital*))). It's a power only a rare few can access and lo and behold, you're one of them. (((*Astral Hospital*))) allows one's astral self to repair any wounds the physical self has sustained, no matter the severity of the wound. Now just lie down and let me patch you the fuck up! And another thing, this time I want you to actually handle Trevyn! He *was* human but now that he's an artificial angel, there is absolutely no need to hold back.

Astral Hellin then used her other-worldly powers to put Hellin back together as if she was never cut in two. Trevyn was completely unaware because the (((*Astral Hospital's*))) second attribute temporarily freezes time around the user. Once completed, Astral Hellin took her leave as Hellin's consciousness slowly returned to the present world. Upon opening her eyes again, Hellin instinctively delivered a robust kick to Trevyn's abdomen, knocking the artificial angel down hard. Springing to her feet, Hellin's hands were suddenly surrounded in a neon red aura. She recalled seeing Onyx do exactly the same with his hands when they faced a dragon, although his hands glowed neon pink. She then remembered the name of this ability, which is called ((((*Psi Fistacuffs*)))). Unsure of how she activated this power, nonetheless her focus reverted to Trevyn, who was back on his feet with the intent to finish her off.

Now on the offense, Hellin rushed at Trevyn with a barrage of fast punches. The artificial angel managed to dodge the first few strikes before Hellin landed a haymaker on his right cheek. Normally, Hellin would have stopped there but after the brutal tongue lashing from her astral self, she showed no mercy as she continued throwing a series of sturdy blows to Trevyn's body. Despite his angelic abilities healing him, due to the exhaustion of the battle, Trevyn was no longer able to continue fighting. Hellin delivered a devastating punch to his gut and he crumpled to the ground. Barely conscious, Trevyn failed to get back on his feet. Hellin knew more hits could prove fatal. She used her telepathy to put Trevyn to sleep. Resisting her demonic urges that screamed at her to rip his head off, Hellin picked Trevyn up off the ground and decided to take him to her friends before going after Love.

While Hellin battled Trevyn, Orsela alongside Starfinder and Lea fought and defeated the mutated Miles brothers. Although the brothers' mutated forms were strong and gave the trio quite a fight, thanks to Orsela's quick thinking, she'd conjured up an attack plan. Combining the skills of Lea, Starfinder, and herself, the trio squelched the brothers before Starfinder put a bullet in each of their heads. Moments later, Hellin returned to her friends with Trevyn in her arms. Though relieved that Hellin was okay and Trevyn was found, seeing his condition, Orsela immediately questioned Hellin.

Orsela: Oh damn, Hellin! Why is Trevyn so beat up?

Lea: You do know the job is to save him, not beat him to a pulp.

Hellin: Shut...the...fuck...up! Trevyn is fine, just sleeping, and he'll heal soon enough. Those fuckers turned him into an Artificial Angel and upon seeing me, he tried to kill me. He almost succeeded, too, but I got lucky somehow and thus, I'm still alive.

Lea: Oh, it's not luck, honey, it's plot armor.

Hellin: Lea, you're going to need fucking plot armor in a minute, bitch! Anyway, now that you three killed those two scientists and I've rescued Trevyn, I'm going to leave him here with you and go find that bitch, Love.

Orsela: Want me to come with you?

Hellin: No need, Orsela. While I doubt you guys will encounter any more trouble, I'd feel better if you stayed with these three. Unlike them, you're the only one here who can still rumble if some shit jumps off while I go looking for that traitorous bitch!

Placing Trevyn in Orsela's arms, Hellin ran off again to find Love. While everyone was battling, Love went after her main target, Dr. Nathaniel Ezekiel. Knowing who sent Love after him, Dr. Ezekiel abandoned his partners without hesitation as he ran deep into his underground laboratory for a place to hide. Being the professional killer that she is, Love was able to find Dr. Ezekiel's hiding spot and cornered him. Immediately, the doctor began begging for his life.

Dr. Ezekiel: No, please don't kill me! I know betraying *him* was not wise but you must understand as a fellow human being, I only did this so we could combat the demons that are taking over our world. Don't you see, if you kill me, you're just helping the demon scourge. We must act now. Together. You and I...we're not like those things! We are the just and rightful inhabitants of *our* precious world. Can't you see, all I want to do is to protect us, and what's rightfully ours, from those damn demons!

Love: Oh, how sad. What a truly sad man. Do you honestly believe us *humans* are better than the demons? If anything, we're worse. Demons are naturally evil, but we humans have a choice. Furthermore, if you truly believe in your crusade against demons, why didn't you use yourself as a test subject for the Artificial Angel ritual instead of kidnapping someone's fucking child? Now that's what I call evil.

Dr. Ezekiel: I'm so, so sorry I kidnapped Trevyn, and accidentally caused the death of his friends. Really, I am. I just knew if I could somehow make the Nigerian Queen's own child a part of our fight to eradicate the demon threat, perhaps...maybe...I could get the Queen on our side, along with others who know the threat demons pose to our world. Just imagine, if we rid the world of demons, we, as humans, will never have to live in fear again.

Love: Oh my, a world without demons... sounds so dreamy. I mean, never mind the dragons, Beasterians*, evil spirits, fairies, other-worldly beings, and most important, the good ol' humans. We just gotta get rid of the demons and life would be just peachy. Then only humans would be the ones carrying out massacres, practicing forbidden magic, kidnapping, and doing other fucked-up shit! I'm a sick bitch and damn proud of it. And I fucking despise a motherfucker who does evil shit then acts as if their actions are righteous! I'm going to enjoy cutting your fucking heart out your chest, you piece of shit!

Dr. Ezekiel: Please don't kill me! I'll give you anything, just please don't kill me! I promise I won't do any more Forbidden experiments if you let me go. I'll even turn myself over to Queen Aliyu, if that's what it takes.

Love: See, if I was under contract to kill you, I would've simply broken both your legs and brought you to my good ol' friend, Hellin. And yes, despite her being a demon, she would have shown you mercy by taking your sorry ass to Queen Aliyu to punish as she sees fit. However, if I don't kill you then I'm going to be killed. That's a no-no! See, Doctor, had you just run off without stealing that Man's secrets, I'm fairly certain he would've let you just live out the rest of your miserable existence in Nigeria. Unfortunately, you made yourself one powerful enemy. One that is not at all forgiving. Therefore, mercy is not a gift I can grant you...even if I wanted to. Now, get ready to show me your inner Scream Queen.

Failing to dissuade the assassin from ending his life, Dr. Ezekiel watched in dread as Love approached him with her signature knife. Not wanting him to make any sound while she killed him, with her knife in hand, Love performed a spell called ((((*Silent Killer*))) that made a small portion of the surrounding area soundproof. Love then torturously stabbed away at Dr. Ezekiel, mutilating his body. Minutes after killing Dr. Ezekiel and holding his heart in her right hand, the door to the room opened. Hellin stood on the other side with her face in its demonic form. She found Love because of the heavy scent of blood along with her natural tracking abilities. Upon seeing Love, Hellin felt the anger of being deceived by her. Hellin rushed over to the assassin and picked her up by her neck. Despite being in Hellin's death grip, Love held firmly onto the dead doctor's heart.

Hellin: You little bitch! I should've killed you a long time ago! I guess now is as good as ever!

Love: Okay, Helly...I get that you're mad at me, and you have every right to be. I played you all like a fiddle back there, but I had a mission to accomplish. I also told you to read my mind.

Hellin: And I told you if you fucked me over that I would fucking end you!

Love: If you're going to kill me, Helly. then that's it, I guess. I can't beat you, so there's no point in me resisting. However, before you do so, please read my mind and see why I did what I did.

Hellin: You have some fucking nerve asking anything of me! Fine, I'll take a peek into that worthless mind of yours! No matter what I see, I'm still going to fucking kill you!

Hellin calmed herself down enough to focus on reading Love's mind. Hellin saw everything that Love had experienced in the past few hours. Despite her anger towards the strawberry blonde assassin, Hellin realized that whoever that *Man* was who hired Love to find and kill Dr. Ezekiel, if Love had failed her mission, he would've hunted her down and killed her too. Although still vexed that Love had deceived her, as an assassin herself, Hellin understood the actions Love took to ensure her mission's success, and felt killing her for that alone would be a waste of a good kill. Hellin released her grip on Love. Love fell ass first to the ground. Now transformed back to her human appearance, Hellin stared at Love with great annoyance as the assassin rose from the floor.

Love: Thanks for sparing me, Hel—

Hellin: Call me Helly. I fucking dare you right about now.

Love: ...Thanks for sparing me, Hellin. I'm truly grateful for it. Now all that's left for me to do is find something to put this fucker's heart inside of until I return to Rogue Town. I'm sorry I deceived Orsela, Starfinder, and *you.*

Hellin: What about Lea?

Love: Oh, fuck her! If I could, I would kill her, too.

Hellin: Touché.

Love: But in all seriousness, I'm sorry, Hellin. And I do hope you were able to save Trevyn. I may not care about him but since he wasn't my target, I have no ill will towards him.

Hellin: Yes, Trevyn is alive and well. He's with the others. Now then, let's go reunite with the rest of the group and get the fuck out of this shithole. I'm ready to go back home.

Love: You can say that again. I miss my mongoose, Lucille, and I'm in desperate need of a shower.

Hellin: One last thing, though, before we go to the others...

Love: And what would that be, Hellin?

Hellin: I want to know more about that Man who hired you. The next time we cross paths, I want some answers. After all, he's the one who created the Forbidden Technique to turn humans into Artificial Angels. Someone like that can prove to be a threat, not only to the Underworld, but even to mortals of this world.

Love: It won't be easy, but I'll definitely fish for information for you before we cross paths again. I'm curious about that bastard as well. Still pissed that he threatened to kill me if I failed. I almost wanted to spare Ezekiel, just to see if he'd make good on his word. Anyway, let's go join the others and leave this shithole, as you said.

The group was surprised when they saw Hellin return with Love...alive. Lea, in particular, was disappointed that Hellin didn't kill her. Not wanting to waste any more time in the laboratory, Hellin sent a telepathic message to both Orsela and Starfinder, promising to explain to them why she spared Love. As for Lea, Hellin simply told her "Get fucked" as she took the still sleeping Trevyn from Orsela and carried him in her arms once again. Once the six of them exited the underground laboratory, Love bade the heroes farewell as she went to meet her contact to help her get out of Nigeria, with Dr. Ezekiel's heart in tow. Meanwhile, Hellin and the others returned to Queen Aliyu's castle.

*Beasterians: Anthropomorphic beings from the state of Beastia, one of the seventy-five states of Mayland. It's predominantly inhabited by lions, tigers, dogs, wolves, bears, bulls, eagles, insects, etc all with very human-like features.

9

Farewell for Now

JOURNEYING back to the castle, the heroes reflected on everything they had gone through thus far.

Lea: I'm so fucking glad that we managed to save Trevyn. If only his friends were so lucky.

Orsela: It's really unfortunate what happened to those two, but at least their souls can rest peacefully now that their murderers paid for their crimes with their lives.

Starfinder: It felt good putting a bullet in each of those assholes' heads. By the way, nice planning back there, Orsela. Who would've guessed Lea's powers would work down there in the laboratory.

Lea: Yeah, I thought I was going to end up turning green and vomiting every thirty minutes by listening to you, but my powers worked just fine in there, and the three of us outsmarted those grotesque bastard scientists.

Orsela: I realized that since they had the anti-tracking spells in the laboratory, that meant the lab was impervious to the anti-teleportation spell that Queen Aliyu placed on Nigeria. Therefore, your powers would work fine down there. That worked to our advantage...big time.

Hellin: I may not always say it, but I absolutely admire your intelligence, Sis.

Orsela: Well, Mom, I mean Queen Othello, made sure that I kept up with my tactical studies. It's one of my many duties back home, after all.

Hellin: Another thing, Orsela... no matter how my...our mother may treat you sometimes, along with Mihoshi, I don't care that you aren't my blood. I see you as my sister. Nothing in this world will ever change that...nothing!

Orsela: Thank you, Hellin. I truly appreciate that more than words could ever describe. I love you.

Hellin: I love you, too.

Lea: Do you guys think I can open a portal from here to Queen Aliyu's castle? All this walking is tiring me out even more than the fight we had earlier.

Hellin: Be my guest. But if you end up turning green and vomiting, don't blame anyone but yourself.

Orsela: I wouldn't advise it, Lea, considering that Queen Aliyu currently has no reason to lift the anti-teleportation spell off Nigeria yet. We still gotta bring her son home to her first.

Starfinder: Besides, we're almost near a town. I'm sure we can find ourselves a Rider to take us back to the castle for free; especially once they see the Prince in Hellin's arms. Speaking of Mr. Sleeping Beauty, don't you think you should wake him up, Hellin?

Hellin: As much as I don't want to carry a 6'2" seventeen-year-old in my arms, I also want Trevyn to get as much rest as possible before bringing him home. Besides, he's far from the heaviest thing I've carried a long distance. Let's just hurry up and reach town and find a damn Rider.

Eventually reaching a small town in Nigeria, the heroes attracted the attention of many people as they rejoiced to see Prince Trevyn was alive, sleeping in Hellin's arms. Without any of them needing to say a word, several Riders rushed to their aid, all offering to be the one to bring them back to Queen Aliyu's castle. While thankful for the generosity of all the Riders, Hellin chose a woman by the name of Oya to take them to rejoin Queen Aliyu.

The two guards standing in front of the castle entrance let Hellin and the others in immediately. Inside, Hellin, with Trevyn still in her arms, made a beeline to the throne room where Queen Aliyu normally resided. Sitting on her throne with a book in hand, Queen Aliyu's heart swelled with unimaginable joy as she saw Hellin move towards her with Trevyn in her arms. The queen quickly approached Hellin. She ordered her servants to bring a bed for Trevyn. A servant dutifully attempted to take the Prince from Hellin's arms while other servants left to retrieve a bed. Hellin insisted upon holding Trevyn. The Princess and the Queen conversed as Orsela, Starfinder, and Lea arrived at the throne room.

Queen Aliyu: Oh, my goodness gracious! You found my baby...but what are these golden circles all over his body?

Hellin: Side effects of the experimentation your son was forced to undergo thanks to that bastard, Ezekiel, and his cronies.

Queen Aliyu: Ezekiel? Are you referring to Nathaniel Ezekiel?

Hellin: That would be the one, Aliyu.

Queen Aliyu: I should've known it was that cretin. I remember when we were kids how much he hated demons and wished that angels would come to eradicate them from Earth. I never imagined the bastard would grow up and kidnap my child. Speaking of which, where is Ezekiel?

Hellin: Dead.

Queen Aliyu: Not that I blame you for killing him but after what he put my people and myself through, I really wish you had brought that bastard back to me alive.

Hellin: I couldn't even if I wanted to, Aliyu. Unfortunately, I wasn't the only one after Ezekiel.

Queen Aliyu: Someone else was gunning for him as well?

Hellin: Sadly, and I'm to blame for trusting her in the first place. While my team and I searched the mountains to locate Trevyn, Love was also in Nigeria. She misled us to believe that she was hired to find Trevyn as well. We later learned that she was, in fact, hired to find and kill Ezekiel.

Queen Aliyu: Love? The Unhappy Ending was in Nigeria? Onyx had told me about that twisted woman. I was so busy worrying about Trevyn that I failed to keep individuals like her out of my country. Well, no use worrying about it now. But tell me, did you make Love pay for her deception?

Hellin: Of course, I wanted to kill that little bitch for lying to me, although most would say it was my fault for not using my telepathy on her. Right before I was going to kill her, she convinced me to read her mind. After what I learned from reading her mind, I decided against it; considering I want to learn more about the son-of-bitch who hired her. While I'm sorry that you didn't get the pleasure of personally punishing Ezekiel, I'm not at all sorry for sparing Love's life.

Queen Aliyu: And they say there's no honor among assassins. Well, the bed's here.

Set my son down. I have more questions regarding what those bastards did to my baby.

After setting Trevyn down on the white bed that was a bit small for him but would have to do in the meantime, Hellin and Orsela explained to Queen Aliyu that Trevyn had been transformed into an Artificial Angel; compliments of a spell Dr. Ezekiel learned in order to turn normal humans into angelic-like beings to hunt and kill demons. Although concerned about what this would mean for her son's future in Nigeria, Queen Aliyu was most thankful that her son was alive. Afterwards, Queen Aliyu instructed her two bodyguards, Rashawn and Vicet, to carry Trevyn to his room to finish resting. Queen Aliyu then asked to speak to Starfinder privately while Hellin and the others waited in the throne room. A short while later, Queen Aliyu and Starfinder returned to the throne room.

Queen Aliyu: Well, now that your business is finished here, Hellin and company, in the next five minutes the anti-teleportation spells my Sages placed throughout Nigeria will no longer be in effect. That means Princess Stallard can teleport the three of you back home.

Hellin: The three of us? Don't you mean four?

Starfinder: No, my dear, three is indeed correct. See, when Queen Aliyu asked me to speak with her in private, she asked if I could stay in Nigeria a little longer. Not only to be Trevyn's temporary bodyguard, until she finds someone worthy of performing the task in my place, but I will also help the lad get used to his newfound powers; especially since both he and I have a similar way of gaining our powers. 'Course, thankfully, Queen Billie didn't force me to become a half-fairy.

Orsela: It was an absolute pleasure traveling and fighting alongside you, August.

Starfinder: The pleasure was mine, ladies. And trust, we shall meet again.

Hellin: Oh, we will, cowboy, and you better make damn sure nothing bad happens to Trevyn while you're in Nigeria...or else. I didn't go through all that bullshit just for some asshole to try to kidnap him again.

Starfinder: I promise I won't let any harm come to the lad.

Lea: We'll, it's not like Trevyn will be defenseless. He is, after all, an Artificial

Angel now. And let's not forget he nearly killed Hellin while under the power's influence.

Queen Aliyu: Speaking of that influence, do I need to worry about Trevyn attacking the demons residing here?

Hellin: While Trevyn was sleeping in my arms, I scanned his mind to make sure he was his normal self. So no, Trevyn shouldn't be going on a demon killing spree once he awakens. However, I do hope that bitch, Nikiema, visits you guys and checks on him... unless her God isn't as all seeing as she claims.

Orsela: Nikiema was probably busy somewhere in China helping Detective Xiaoyu, but I'm sure she's aware of what happened here and should be making an appearance soon.

Lea: Anyway, it's been five minutes, ladies. Well, Nigeria's been fun, but I think it's time we get going back to Mayland.

Queen Aliyu: Oh, I, too, am happy you're ready to leave Nigeria, Princess Stallard. Try not to come back too soon, dear. As for you, Hellin and Orsela, thank you once again for bringing my son back home to me. I'm forever grateful to both of you ladies.

Hellin: I'm just glad Trevyn is back home where he belongs. Okay, Lea, get ready to take the three of us back to Mayland. I need to check on Onyx first before returning home to Babylon.

Lea's eyes changed from silver to multicolored as she opened a portal for Hellin, Orsela, and herself inside of the throne room. Hellin and Orsela waved farewell to Queen Aliyu as the three women exited Nigeria en route to Mayland.

10

Thank You for Being You

HELLIN, with Orsela and Lea trailing behind her, appeared in front of Onyx's castle in the Royal Lands, after leaving Nigeria. They headed straight to the castle entrance without hesitation. Hellin struck down the door with a single punch. Walking over the door, Hellin found herself confronted by the entirety of Onyx's guards. Orsela and Lea, running in behind her, weren't surprised to see Onyx's guards in fight mode; especially after Hellin unnecessarily knocked down the door. Seconds later, James, Anna, and Yura appeared alongside the guards to confront Hellin and company.

Yura: What the hell is your problem, Strongs! I always knew you'd be a problem someday. I just didn't think it would be today.

Anna: Nonetheless, we're more than happy to kick your sorry ass, along with Orsela and Lea, if they're in on this shit attempt of an ambush.

Lea: Hey, slow the fuck down, orange head! First, neither Orsela nor I know why Hellin even punched the damn door down instead of knocking. Besides, you do know I could literally just teleport the three of us out of here if I wanted, right?

James: Then why the fuck did you punch the door down, Hellin?

Hellin: Ask that *bitch* why I punched the door down.

James, Anna, and the rest of Onyx's guards swiftly realized she was talking about Yura, and all turned to look at her. Remembering her last interaction with Hellin over the phone and how rudely she dismissed her, Yura sighed before explaining to her comrades why Hellin was being more of a bitch than usual.

Yura: I know why Hellin is pissed off, and at me specifically. However, that doesn't give you the damn right to punch the King's door down like some damn neanderthal.

Hellin: Fuck that door! Where's Onyx?

James: Since when do you give two fucks about what's going on with Onyx?

Hellin: I gave a fuck the moment he aided me in finding Trevyn; only for me to lose all contact with him afterwards in the Astral Plane. Something happened to Onyx and I'm here to find out what. Someone better give me some goddamn answers or fucking heads will roll!

Before the situation between Hellin and the protectors of Onyx's castle escalated, Onyx appeared at the top of the stairs in his see-through pink house robe with a bowl of white chocolate raspberry and truffle ice cream in hand. Unaware of the commotion that happened prior, Onyx looked down and noticed the door to the entrance of his castle had been destroyed. Ignoring it, he turned his attention to Hellin. Upon seeing her, Onyx lept from the stairs and landed in front of James, Yura, Anna, and the others with his ice cream still in hand. The king then giddly made his way over to Hellin.

Onyx: Hellin! You're back from Nigeria. Oh, hello Orsela and Lea. I take it that Trevyn was found and is back with his loving mother.

Hellin: Fuck all that! What the hell happened to you back in the Astral Plane?

Onyx: OMG, I didn't think you would even care, to be quite honest. Well, since you're so concerned about what happened when we lost contact, don't you recall me telling you about the ramifications of us using the Forbidden Spell to find Trevyn?

Hellin: Yeah, I recall you saying something about ramifications. So exactly what the hell happened to you?

Onyx: Oh, nothing major, just fell into a coma for a while. Thankfully, my mind repaired itself and voila, I'm all better now. I woke up hungry, so I grabbed some ice cream out of my mini fridge in my room, and came out to tell my subjects the good news.

Hellin: So, you risked going into a coma just to save Trevyn?

Onyx: And it was well worth it!

Orsela: That definitely sounds like the Onyx we know and love.

Lea: What king puts his own life in jeopardy to save someone's son?

Onyx: Queen Aliyu is a good friend of mine, and I have known Trevyn since he was an infant. I couldn't forgive myself if something bad happened to him, knowing that I didn't use all the resources at my disposal.

Hellin: True, but using a Forbidden Spell... that's quite a fucking gamble, don't you think?

Onyx: It fucking worked out in the end so... Oh, my ice cream is starting to melt, and you all know how much I hate eating melted ice cream. Hellin, follow me to the backyard. Meanwhile, Orsela and Lea, make yourselves comfortable. Oh and, James, kindly fix the door.

James: Why me? Hellin broke it.

Onyx: James... fix the door please.

James: I'm on it, bestie.

Anna: I'll help you, Dad.

James: Thanks, Daughter.

Hellin followed Onyx to the backyard where she and Orsela had been teleported to Blue Jay City. The two went over to the swing set in the middle of the yard, and took a seat on each swing. Once seated, they enjoyed the sunset for a few moments before beginning their conversation.

Onyx: I don't know how to explain it but while I was dreaming, in my coma, I had this dream of you rescuing me.

Hellin: Whenever I see you in my dreams, I consider them nightmares.

Onyx: Oh, really? What kind of monster am I in those bad dreams of yours? Am I the mysterious Sage, leading you to an oven to cook you for dinner or—

Hellin: The fucking annoying type just like you're being now. Please tell me you didn't bring me back here just for mindless chit chat.

Onyx: You and I know that's definitely not the case, but it would be nice to have a conversation with you on lighter matters. Sadly, you don't want that type of friendship with me, Hellin. Thankfully, as demons, we have a very, very long time to live. Hopefully, you'll come to like me as much as I like you someday. Still, I'm thankful you were concerned about my well-being. I honestly didn't think you would care what happened to me as long as you found Trevyn.

Hellin: Onyx... do you recall the day my mother introduced the two of us?

Onyx: Well, it was only two hundred and twenty-five years ago but sure, I remember.

Hellin: The first time I laid eyes on you, my heart sank. It was like looking in a mirror, minus the few similarities I share with my mother. Ever since that day, I despised you. Regardless of how much of a bitch I've been to you, never once has your heart grown sour towards me.

Onyx: Hey, it's not like I don't pester the hell out of you, Hellin. All the errands you run for me in Mayland despite your home realm being the Underworld. Sometimes I feel... well actually, a lot of times I feel your scorn is the least of what I should be receiving from you. I'm still waiting for the day you just walk up to me and punch me dead in the face.

Hellin: I had that urge of punching, no killing, you more times than I wish to count, Onyx. Sadly, the only thing that stops me from acting on those feelings is my mother.

Onyx: Now, you and I know that's a lie. If you wanted to harm me, Hellin, nothing short of Satan himself would stop you. I think it's because the two of us share a special connection. Almost as if hurting the other is like hurting oneself.

Hellin: Speaking of hurting oneself, why the fuck didn't you tell me that Lea was going to be our teleporter?

Onyx: Okubi wasn't available and other than Lea, there was no teleporter I trusted enough for this mission. She may be a bitch, but Lea was the woman for the job.

Hellin: Sadly, I can't say I disagree, but it would've been nice if you gave me a heads-up.

Onyx: As if you would've been any happier if you knew before you arrived in Texas.

Hellin: Damn, we really been in each other's lives for a very long time.

Onyx: I wish we've known each other even longer than that. Honestly, I can't explain it but until I met you, Hellin, I never realized how incomplete I felt in life. While James and later, Yura, have always been there for me, it's just something about you that makes me feel whole... even if we are two different beings.

Hellin: I sometimes wonder how different the two of us really are. Our powers are basically the same and of course, our appearance is practically identical.

Onyx: Well, my eyes are blue-green and turquoise. Yours are red like a typical demon. I also can summon the Mariana Trench. You can't, but you have much better control over fire than I ever will. Anyways, I don't want to waste too much more of your time, Hellin. I mainly bought you back here to ease the tension between my guards and you. Also, I wanted to thank you just for being you.

Hellin: Why do you say that exactly?

Onyx: I'm just happy you had the same drive to find Trevyn as I did. I have many strong allies, Hellin, but none compare to you. So once again, thank you for being you.

Hellin: No problem, Onyx. Despite how I still feel about you and my overall feelings for Mayland, I do care what happens to this realm and the citizens residing here. I just pray the day never comes where I have to choose between Mayland and the Under-world because we *both* know which one I'll choose.

Onyx: As long as you know which one I will choose then we're good, but I, too, hope that day never comes. I cherish you as an ally and dread you as an enemy. Anyways, Hellin, it's time I get Orsela and you back to the Underworld. I'm pretty sure Lea will end up spending the night before going back to Plutonia in the morning.

Hellin: Well, it was good talking to you, Onyx, and thank you for being you as well.

Onyx and Hellin shared a mutual smile of respect before Hellin hopped off the swing and headed back to retrieve Orsela. Minutes later, both women returned to the backyard as Onyx opened a portal that led to the Underworld. Orsela and Onyx kissed and hugged and said their farewells for now. Onyxe watched as the women stepped into the portal before it disappeared. Grateful to have an ally in Hellin, he cried tears of joy for a few moments. The king then wiped his face and went back inside his castle.

Hellin and Orsela returned to Babylon and were immediately greeted by Queen Othello and her servants. Othello walked up to her daughter and placed a kiss on her forehead. She patted Orsela on her head for a job well done. Othello then ordered her girls to follow to partake in the meal she had her chefs prepare to celebrate their success. At first, Hellin and Orsela were confused by the dinner since their mother wouldn't have a clue if they were successful or not. Othello, having read their thoughts, replied, "Well, you're back home, so that's proof of success to me." The girls just give her an awkward look before proceeding to the dining table.

Waiting at the table was an array of Underworld delicacies along with an irritated Mihoshi already seated. Hellin made brief eye contact with her older sister. Both women did little to hide their animosity towards each other, yet both knew better than to act up in front of their mother. The servants pulled out seats for Othello, Hellin, and Orsela before all four women began to feast.

Othello: So, tell Mommy all about your successful mission.

Orsela: Well, Your Majesty, we were able to successfully find and rescue Trevyn. He's safely at home with his mother, Queen Aliyu. Starfinder stayed behind to train the lad to use his new powers.

Mihoshi: Pretty sure Mom was talking to Hellin and not you, Orsela.

Hellin: Well, she didn't specify, Mihoshi, that she was talking to me and all three of us at this table are her daughters.

Mihoshi: Even if she only gave birth to two of us. Or, the fact that only one of us was made the natural way—

Hellin: An adopted child is still a child and should not be treated any different. And it's an honor to be a special baby instead of being conceived in the boring traditional way. But you would know all about boring right, Mihoshi?

Othello: Girls, behave yourselves. And yes, while I was referring to Hellin, I'm grateful my daughter, Orsela, had an answer. Now, Hellin, may I hear from you? What happened on your latest mission?

Hellin: No need to repeat what Orsela has already said, but she did leave out one thing that I feel could become an issue. We did find Trevyn and bring him safely back to his mother. Unfortunately, the bastards who kidnapped him turned him into an Artificial Angel. When I first found Trevyn, because of the effect of his experimentation, he tried to kill me and nearly succeeded.

Mihoshi: Only nearly? Too bad.

Hellin: I doubt you would've been so lucky, Moe. Fortunately, the bastards responsible for turning Trevyn into an Artificial Angel were dealt with, although Love was the one who killed the ringleader, Dr. Nathaniel Ezekiel. Orsela, Lea, and Starfinder took down his cronies, Alec and Richard Miles.

Othello: What exactly was so hard about taking down scientists?

Orsela: Well, Ezekiel, from what I saw, was a piece of cake for Love. The Miles brothers had injected themselves with some serum that mutated them into hulk-like monsters.

Hellin: But Orsela, being the smart little cookie she is, cooked up a strategy alongside Starfinder and Lea to kill the Miles brothers.

Mihoshi: Anyone Orsela could outsmart deserves to die.

Othello: Sounds like a rather dangerous mission, to be quite honest. Nonetheless, it was a job well done. I'll have something interesting to tell my fellow Demon Lords tomorrow, concerning the threat of folks in the Mortal Realm making Artificial Angels. Thankfully, the process of turning a person into an Artificial Angel only has one in a fifty percent chance. Still, anyone who possesses such information should be dealt with swiftly.

Hellin: I couldn't agree more, Mother.

Othello: Well, I am just happy to have my favorite girls with me for this delicious dinner. Orsela, don't forget to feed Mr. Perentie for me after you finish eating.

Orsela: Yes, your—

Othello: Just call me Mother right now, dear. Save the formalities for another time.

Othello and her daughters finished enjoying their dinner before getting ready for the night as the women of the Strongs Household prepared for yet another day. Bearing in mind her deal with Love back in Nigeria, Hellin decided to let her mother speak to the other Demon Lords regarding the creation of Artificial Angels before making any other moves for now. After dinner, Hellin waited for Orsela to feed Mr. Perentie. The two women then headed to their room for the night. Hellin exercised for a while as she reflected on her conversation with Onyx. Orsela read a book about Nox Monsters. Both women finally decided it was time for bed.

BONUS
SHORT
STORIES

ONYXE BLADE

ORSELA vs NOX ASRAI

A WEEK after the events in Nigeria, the trio of Hellin, Orsela, and Onyx hung out together on the King's day off in the state of Magius, one of the seventy-five states in Mayland. Magius was a magical place known for its vibrant buildings and openly sexual citizens (just don't assume all of Magius' residents swing both ways). Hellin, who normally despised being any place in Mayland, decided to join Orsela and Onyx on their little trip to the newest mall that had opened in Magius; mainly because she didn't want to be stuck at home with her mother who was indulging in the company of a male or three. And she didn't want to be around Mihoshi any more than necessary. Thus, she decided to hang with Orsela and her Onyx whom she still disliked but had grown to tolerate.

The trio exited the mall as Orsela and Onyx ate peach cobbler ice cream from the ever-popular Minty's Ice Cream parlor. Hellin drank a can of blueberry soda from a vending machine because she didn't have much of an appetite... at least for mortal food. They walked around and enjoyed the scenery as Orsela and Onyx finished their ice cream. The trio finally found a bench and sat near Nectar Park.

Orsela: This new mall sure is beautiful, Onyx. Thanks for inviting Hellin and me to come hangout with you today.

Onyx: No problem, Orsela. That goes for you too, Hellin.

Hellin: Don't think too much about it, jackass! I'm only here to be with my sister. That and the fact that I didn't want to be stuck in the house right now. I still hate being in Mayland and I still don't care too much to be around you, either.

Onyx: Oh, and to think I thought we were close, Hellin; especially after that talk we had a week ago in my backyard.

Orsela: Oh yeah, I meant to ask you guys what did you talk about?

Hellin: Nothing important. And yes, Onyx, we had a moment but my overall feelings towards you haven't changed. My mother still refuses to share whatever connection we have with each other, and you not knowing either doesn't make things any better.

Onyx: And you hold me responsible for those unanswered questions?

Hellin: Oh whatever, Your Majesty! Besides, now that our trip to the mall is over, isn't it about time you open up a portal for us back to Babylon and you return to your kingdom? I doubt Yura wants to substitute as ruler of Mayland for too long.

Onyx: Oh, you'd be surprised how well Yura can operate in my absence. Besides, don't you two want to go with me to visit Romeo and Rodrigo at Beastia?

Orsela: I would love to go to Beastia. I haven't seen those two in a good minute.

Hellin: I'll pass on seeing himbo lion and barely clothed tiger, thank you.

Orsela: Oh c'mon, Hellin, don't be like that. It's not like we need to get back to Babylon so soon.

Onyx: Yeah, Hellin, don't be such a—

Before Onyx could finish his sentence, the cellphone in his vest pocket rang.

Onyx: Hey, Yura, what's up?

Hellin and Orsela watched as Onyx's facial expressions quickly indicated that something was wrong. Onyx told Yura he would handle it as he hung up the phone on his right-hand lady. He then turned his attention over to Hellin and Orsela once again.

Onyx: Hey, there's a situation at the Abidel Lake located in Tishman City. I'll open a portal for you two first back to Babylon then I'll investigate the situation in Tishman.

Orsela: Are you sure you don't need any help, Onyx?

Hellin: It's not like we have anything better to do.

Onyx: No, it's alright, Orsela, but I appreciate the offer. And, Hellin, I don't want to intrude on your personal time. After all, don't want you to have to hang around me any longer than you must.

Hellin: Geez, where the fuck is this attitude coming from? You're usually all chipper and shit.

Orsela: Well, Hellin, how long do you think you can be a bitch towards the man without him becoming fed up?

Hellin glared at Orsela. Instead of backing down, Orsela glared back at her. Turning her head to Onyx, she was surprised to see him looking at her in utter annoyance. Realizing that she was in the wrong, Hellin sighed as she turned to Onyx.

Hellin: Okay, I know I can be a real piece of work sometimes but if you don't mind, Onyx, Orsela and I would love to come with you to Tishman City. Afterwards you can open a portal for us to go back home.

Onyx: Okay, fine, it's not like I have time to waste arguing.

Rising off the bench, Onyx held his hands out and opened a portal for Hellin, Orsela, and himself to exit Magius and enter Tishman City.

Within seconds, the trio appeared in the Abidel Forest, not too far from the Abidel Lake. Upon their arrival, they saw several Sages lying unconscious on the ground. Three of the unconscious Sages were policemen. Immediately, Onyx and Orsela rushed to their aid while Hellin used her telepathy to sense any nearby enemies. Noticing that one of the police officers was semi-conscious, Onyx approached her and used his telepathy to read her mind. Seeing what happened through the woman's memories, the king learned that some creature at the lake had attacked several Sages training in the area. She, along with her partners, came to investigate and met with the same fate. Realizing that all the Sages on the ground were soaking wet, it didn't take too many brain cells to figure out the creature that attacked them wielded water-based powers.

Onyx turned to Hellin to see if she sensed anything. Hellin nodded towards Abidel Lake, indicating that she sensed some sought of life-form there. Knowing what they had to do, the trio hurried over to Abidel Lake to uncover exactly what had attacked the Sages.

Reaching their destination, Onyx used his water-based powers to check for signs of life within the lake. Despite his best efforts, nothing unusual could be detected.

Onyx: This is rather odd. Hellin, you said you sensed something in the lake.

Hellin: Are you fucking calling me a liar?

Onyx: No, that's not what I said dammit! It just doesn't make sense that nothing is appearing inside the lake.

Hellin: Perhaps it's your powers acting up... because I know what I sense here.

Onyx: Well, perhaps it's true that you're a shitty telepath, Hellin.

Hellin: Excuse you!

Orsela: Can you two please just stop arguing! I swear we've known each other over two hundred years and you two can't for—

Both her Nox cards, Valerie and Macky, started to glow intensely inside her pockets, which signaled to their master that they were in the domain of a Nox monster. Before Orsela could tell Hellin and Onyx what she realized, two gigantic watery hands suddenly popped out from the lake and struck Hellin and Onyx, sending the two crashing to the ground. Shocked by the unexpected attack on her friends, Orsela then saw a woman made of water wearing a crown and a loose white gown, standing in the lake. Recognizing this creature from her Nox book back home, she looked on in horror as she faced one of the legendary Nox monsters known as Nox Asrai! The Nox monster then raised her right hand and made a magical barrier behind Orsela that separated her from Hellin and Onyx. Sensing the creature knew she was a Nox Tamer, Orsela acknowledged that she posed the greatest threat to her, and Nox Asrai challenged her to a one-on-one fight.

Hellin and Onyx quickly recovered from the assault. They were startled to see a barrier in front of them, but no Orsela in sight. Angrily, Hellin attempted to run up to the barrier, but Onyx grabbed her by the leg.

Hellin: Onyx, what in the fuck are you doing? We gotta go help Orsela!

Onyx: Hellin, do you not realize what's going on here? The barrier happens when a Nox Tamer is being confronted by a wild Nox. We cannot interfere unless we want to risk Orsela losing her connection with the Nox creatures, including the ones she already possesses.

Hellin: So, what the fuck do we do then? Just wait here and hope Orsela will be alright?

Onyx: Orsela is as tough as they come and smart as a whip. I'm fairly certain she can handle this battle on her own. Besides, she's not exactly alone with both her Nox monsters in her possession. Now just have some damn faith and trust that your sister got this fight in the bag.

Orsela: Okay, Nox Asrai, I know what you're capable of. Not only am I going to defeat you, I'm going to add you to my collection! Now get ready to feel the wrath of Orsela Geno!

Orsela charged at Nox Asrai using her superhuman agility as Nox Asrai unleashed a series of water blasts at her. Dodging the attacks, Orsela planned a strategy to defeat the watery Nox creature. Intensifying her assault, Nox Asrai created a twister and hurled it at her target. Orsela, stunned by the sight of the twister, attempted to dodge it, but was caught. The twister bombarded her and spun her body around within it. Orsela, being a demon, was able to endure the pain. The twister disbursed and Orsela fell hard to the ground. Soaked and hurt but far from defeated, Orsela decided it was time to use one of her Nox monsters. She immediately summoned Nox Macky, an alien psychic and muscular boxer, to battle alongside her.

Orsela: Okay, Nox Macky, let's show Nox Asrai that her powers can't match our teamwork. Now, Macky, let's rush her ass!

Following his master's orders, Nox Macky and Orsela charged at Nox Asrai. The watery Nox monster continued her watery assault. Because of the mental link between Orsela and Nox Macky, they managed to avoid the intense water blasts and moved into striking range. Realizing that she was unable to keep her two foes at bay, Nox Asrai created a shield of water to protect herself. Nox Asrai was not fast enough as Orsela and Nox Macky both struck her in the gut. The monster crumbled to her knees inside of the lake. While Orsela would have liked to have shown Nox Asrai mercy, she knew the only way to end the battle was to knock out the monster.

Orsela signaled to Nox Macky to deliver one more devastating punch to Nox Asrai's face, which knocked out the monster inside the lake. The barrier that separated Orsela from the others began to fade. Nox Asrai's body transformed into a blue card. Orsela plucked it out the lake. She then gave Nox Macky a kiss on his forehead before he reverted back into a card. Placing both Nox monsters inside her pocket, Orsela waited for the barrier to completely dissolve before running over to Hellin and Onyx.

Orsela: Man, am I glad to see the two of you.

Hellin: I'm just happy you're okay. I was worried when that damn thing separated us from you. Thankfully, Onyx was here with his wisdom to keep me from doing something stupid,

Onyx: I wouldn't have thought that a Nox monster was responsible for attacking all these people at the lake. Thankfully, while you were busy with your fight, I, along with Hellin's help, opened a portal to get all the unconscious folks to a nearby hospital.

Orsela: I'm happy to hear you two worked together while I was busy catching myself a new Nox monster.

Hellin: Well, we had... wait, did you catch it?

Orsela: Of course, Hellin. Wanna have a look?

Hellin: Hell yeah!

Orsela reached in her pocket and pulled out three Nox monster cards; two being Nox Macky and Nox Valerie, which she already owned, along with her newly acquired Nox Asrai card. Hellin, proud of her sister's latest accomplishment, gave her a big hug. Now that the situation in Tishman City had been handled, Onyx thanked the girls for their service then opened a portal for them to return home to Babylon.

THE HOLY BLADE OF NIGERIA

TREVYN squeezed his favorite agave pine-apple body wash onto his red satin wash cloth and began his morning shower. After finishing up in the shower, he grabbed his mahogany towel off the bathroom reel and dried off. He brushed and flossed his teeth before sliding on his red Marvy Zayn boxers then returned to his room. Once dressed for the day, Trevyn headed downstairs to greet his mother, Queen Aliyu, in her throne room, and gave her a good morning kiss on the cheek.

Queen Aliyu: Hey, young man, where are you off to in such a hurry? Don't you want to eat the delicious breakfast prepared by our chefs?

Trevyn: I'll skip breakfast, at least here, Mom. I'm going to meet up with August at the back of the castle to get in more training. Then we're going to Lagos. We'll get something to eat while we're there, but please make sure the chefs cook my favorite meal for dinner tonight.

Queen Aliyu: Sure thing. I must say you seem to have grown quite fond of Mr. Starfinder.

Trevyn: Hey, Mom, don't make it sound so weird. It's just nice to have someone around other than you who doesn't look at me so strange; especially since these golden rings tattooed on my body are permanent. Thanks to what those assholes back at Eket did to me.

Queen Aliyu: I'm just glad Nikiema finally made her way to Nigeria that night after Hellin, Orsela, and Lea went home. Because she's an actual angel, despite having a foul mouth that rivals Hellin's, she was able to stabilize your artificial angelic powers so they don't backfire on you down the line. Also, I meant nothing weird about my comment regarding you and Starfinder. Besides, I honestly wouldn't care if you two were a thing.

Trevyn: Thanks, Mom, but that's definitely not the case. I may be legal, but I'm still seventeen. Starfinder is a few years older than you. I do not want my first time to be with someone that old. As for Nikiema... I appreciate what she did for me, but I didn't like how she made it seem like Hellin made a bad call. I'm still heated that she thought it would've been better for Hellin to seek out her help than to search for me without her help. Like, bitch, I could've possibly ended up worse than what I am if Hellin and the others didn't find me when they did.

Queen Aliyu: I agree that Nikiema tends to overstate her importance in the situation; considering she was busy helping Nara and Detective Xiaoyu investigate an incident in Japan. We didn't have the luxury of waiting around for her when you went missing. Regardless, I'm just glad you're home and safe and, most importantly, seem to have control over your powers. Anyway, I held you up long enough. I'm pretty sure Mr. Starfinder is more than ready to start your training for the day; especially since he's going back to Texas after tonight.

Trevyn: Oh man, it's already been a week since everything happened! Yeah, I better go enjoy what time I have left with August before he heads back to Mayland... well, Texas, which is located in Mayland.

Trevyn gave his mother another kiss on the cheek before leaving to meet up with Starfinder at the back of the castle. Trevyn spotted Starfinder smoking a cigar near the maple tree. Shaking his head, as he couldn't understand why anyone would smoke those damn things, Trevyn decided to ignore it as he called out to Starfinder.

Trevyn: Good morning, cowboy.

Starfinder: Howdy, Trevyn.

Trevyn: Oh cool, you finally got used to calling me just Trevyn and not Prince Trevyn. I'm glad because no one I consider a true friend has to address me by my title.

Starfinder: Thanks for being so comfortable with me calling you just Trevyn.

Trevyn: Besides, you don't call Hellin, Princess Hellin, Onyx, King Onyx, or Lea, Princess Stallard every time you speak to one of them, so why not just call me Trevyn?

Starfinder: Okay, kid, I didn't need a whole breakdown just to call you Trevyn. Anyway, let's cut the chit chat. You need more training before we head to Lagos. Yesterday you seemed to have a better understanding of how to use your angelic powers by creating blades of light. However, it seems to me, you're more suited to use your powers another way; sought of like a boxer, if you ask me.

Trevyn: Really? You're not just saying that because of how I'm dressed?

Starfinder: They say not to judge a book by its cover, but you're definitely giving brawler vibes, my handsome friend. So, I want to see if you can infuse your light powers into your fist instead of making blades of light. And that's not to say making light blades ain't cool or useful. I just think learning how to infuse your powers with your physical strength will prove more beneficial for you.

Trevyn: Okay, sounds fair enough. Let's give it a shot.

The golden halo tattoos on Trevyn's body started glowing as he began manifesting his angelic powers into his fist. Within seconds, his hands were covered in white light.

Trevyn: Oh shit, it worked!

Starfinder: Now let's put your powers to the test, kiddo.

Trevyn: About that, can it wait? It's not like we haven't been training all this week. This being your last night here in Nigeria, I really want to show you around Lagos.

Starfinder: I've been to Lagos before, kid, pretty sure there ain't nothing new you can show me over there.

Trevyn: Oh, trust me, you'd be surprised by all the cool places my friends and I... yeah, maybe it's not a good idea.

Starfinder: It seems you still haven't gotten over your survivor's guilt.

Trevyn: As much as I'm happy to be alive and my mother is able to run Nigeria relatively smooth, I can't help but feel bad about Jamaal and Alimi's deaths.

Starfinder: You gotta stop beating yourself up for that, kid. It's not your fault what happened to your friends. Just be grateful you're alive to carry the memory of them inside your heart.

Trevyn: Ever since I returned home to my mother, Alimi's family stopped speaking to us and Jamaal's father decided to leave Nigeria to go live in France. It's like I'm somehow the blame for their passing, and it makes me feel bad, August.

August put out his cigar and walked over to Trevyn. He gave the young lad a hug and told him not to blame himself; Dr. Ezekiel and his cohorts killed his friends. In an effort to cheer Trevyn up, Starfinder asked him to show him around Lagos; especially some good places to eat since neither of them had breakfast yet. Trevyn was excited to hear the enthusiasm in Starfinder's voice, as well as being hungry himself. The two of them searched for a Rider to take them to Lagos.

After enjoying a wonderful day together hanging out in Lagos, the two men saw the sun begin to set and decided it was a good time to start heading back to the castle. Less than a half hour away from home, Trevyn and Starfinder relished the beautiful peace of the quiet roads as they savored the ride.

Suddenly, they heard a girl scream within the forest across the road. Without warning, Trevyn's halo tattoos glowed. He ran out the Rider's wagon, leaving Starfinder behind, and he instinctively used his (((Holy Rush))) technique. Making his way into the forest minutes later, Trevyn spotted a tall and muscular Nigerian man dressed in a true blue and black dashiki. Standing across from him were two young girls. The older one was obviously human, but the younger one was a Cambion, with the physical appearance of a demon. The older girl held her little sister protectively in her arms. Trevyn quickly realized what was going on, and he didn't like it one bit.

Trevyn: Ayo! Leave those two girls alone. Go find some tree to jerk off behind!

Nigerian Man: Well, if it isn't the Prince himself. What are you doing all out alone this time of the day? Trying to get yourself kidnapped again?

Trevyn: Dude, I don't give two fucks about your opinion of me. I know one damn thing for certain is you're going to leave those girls alone. Or you'll soon find out that the Prince of Nigeria ain't nothing to mess with.

Nigerian Man: If you must, you can take the human girl back wherever she came from, but the half-breed stays here for extermination.

Trevyn: Are you deaf or dumb? I said leave them both alone!

Nigerian Man: Why don't you mind your damn business, Momma's boy! Run on home before I make an example of you!

Trevyn: Okay, asshole, if you're so bad then state your name.

Nigerian Man: My name is Monreau, and I despise demons and fools like you who want to protect them. These vermin must be...

Trevyn: Okay, bigot, I didn't ask for a damn speech. I just wanted to know the name of the person whose ass I'm about to kick!

Monreau: Insolent boy! Your bloodline shall *end* with you!

(((Blue Extermination)))

Monreau created a gigantic blast of blue fire in his palm before throwing it at Trevyn. Using his angelic powers, Trevyn surrounded his body in a holy light right before the blast of fire struck him, which nullified the attack completely. Trevyn then held his arms to his sides, staring at Monreau with anger in his eyes. The Nigerian sage looked at Trevyn in terror as he realized he bit off more than he could chew.

Trevyn: You had your chance. Now you're going to feel the wrath of an Artificial Angel!

Covering both his hands in light energy, Trevyn used his superhuman speed and appeared right in front of Monreau in a split second. Before Monreau had a chance to react, Trevyn struck him with Holy energy jabs in the stomach. After a few well-placed strikes, Monreau went down for the count.

Once he defeated the bigoted Sage, Trevyn went over to check on the two young girls. They were as happy to be saved by him as he was to rescue them. Starfinder appeared in the forest a few seconds later with his guns out. The two girls were again frightened, but Trevyn quickly calmed them down as he revealed to them that the brightly dressed cowboy was his friend and mentor. Seeing Monreau's unconscious body on the ground, Starfinder was fairly certain what happened, but asked Trevyn anyway.

Starfinder: So, this clown lying all beaten up on the ground, what did he do to deserve an ass kicking from you?

Trevyn: Jackass was targeting this little Cambion girl here, and her brave big sister never left her side. They must've been playing in the forest when they encountered that asshole down on the ground. I'm just glad we were at the right place at the right time.

Starfinder: I'm damn proud of you, Trevyn. You really got the hang of your angelic powers pretty fast.

Trevyn: All thanks to you, teach.

Trevyn and Starfinder gave each other a smile of respect before Starfinder picked Monreau off the ground and placed him under a nearby tree. Then he pulled out a pair of anti-magic cuffs and bound the unconscious Sage's hands together.

Starfinder: Okay, now that this fucker can't cause any more trouble, let's get these little ladies home. Then we'll tell your mom about this incident so she can send her men to fetch this asswipe. Man, it's been one helluva day.

Trevyn: A day I won't soon forget.

ADEWALE'S CHOICE

A WEEK had passed since he'd betrayed his Queen and country. A once respected Sage and proud protector of Nigeria, he'd turned his back on his Queen because of his disdain for her laws welcoming demons into Nigeria. Upon his defeat by the dual efforts of Hellin and Queen Aliyu, the great wind Sage, Adewale Osefo, now sat in a cell inside the castle dungeons with an anti-magic color around his neck.

Wearing nothing but a black jumpsuit, he pulled down the upper part of the outfit to expose his muscular physique. He spent his days exercising in his cell and reading the same five books over and over. He wondered why hadn't Queen Aliyu already have him executed. He certainly knew she would never forgive his actions towards her and Nigeria, and that she had many slain for crimes less severe than his. So why exactly was he still alive? Perhaps Trevyn was the one convincing his mother to hold off killing him. No, that can't be. Trevyn never much cared for him and preferred Vicet and Rashawn over him. *So, why am I still alive?*, the disgraced Sage wondered as the guard brought his breakfast of bananas, oat biscuits, coconut water, sliced turkey, and cashews. Upon completing his breakfast, Adewale lay on his cot and pondered why he had yet to be executed for his crimes.

The guard unexpectedly returned; too quickly to remove the breakfast tray. She gave Adewale a look that you give to someone you wish dead. Staring at him a bit longer, the guard said to him, "Get off your ass. Someone is here to see you." Believing that Queen Aliyu had finally made her decision on his punishment, Adewale rose from his bed as he prepared himself for whatever awaited him.

To his shock and horror, when the guard opened his cell door, it was not Queen Aliyu or any of the loyal guards, but Mayland's very own King Onyx; wearing his typical pink threads and a calm look on his face. Adewale stared at King Onyx with hatred in his eyes, believing that Onyx was ultimately to blame for Queen Aliyu allowing demons in Nigeria with open arms. However, with his anti-magic collar on, along with the fact that King Onyx was much stronger than him, Adewale knew he didn't stand a chance. Once inside the cell with Adewale, Onyx instructed the guard to close the cell and allow him and Adewale some privacy. The guard obliged the king as she walked off, hoping that Onyx was there to kill him.

Onyx: So, you're the troublemaker my dear friend, Aliyu, told me about when she and I last spoke on the phone.

Adewale: What are you doing here? Are you here to rape me? Turn me into a Darken*? No, I get it now... you're going to eat me alive like the monster you are!

Onyx: Or better yet, all the above. After all, for your betrayal to your Queen, it's the very least you deserve, my dear. Wonder how good you're going to taste in my mouth. But first, you're a bit too tall for me, so how about I put you on your knees?

Using his telepathic powers, Onyx forced Adewale to his knees. The King then got down on all fours and crawled menacingly towards the defenseless Sage. Once in front of Adewale, Onyx lunged his face towards Adewale's neck. Adewale ignored his instinct to flinch in order not to show visible fear to what he thought was about to happen. Onyx motioned as if he was going to bite Adewale's neck, only to merely give him a playful peck instead. Still toying with the frightened man, Onyx moved down to his chest area and seductively licked his nipple. Uncomfortable and terrified by the demon's actions, Adewale murmured, "Please stop toying with me and just finish me off. At least let me die with my dignity." Seeing fear in Adewale's face, Onyx couldn't help but look at him in disappointment.

Onyx: Oh, you're no fun. I guess I may as well give you a quick death then. Say a prayer to your maker, you filthy traitor!

Adewale closed his eyes, expecting Onyx to rip out his heart or intestines. Instead, while Adewale's eyes were closed, Onyx removed the anti-magic collar from around his neck.

Onyx: Okay, I "killed" you, Adewale. You can open your eyes now. I'm just kidding... you're obviously not dead, so just open your eyes, Sir.

Confused, Adewale hesitantly opened his eyes and, to his surprise, saw Onyx holding the anti-magic collar in his left hand.

Adewale: What... wait! Did you just remove my collar? But why? Do you not realize that now, within a few seconds, I will regain access to my magic?

Onyx: Yes, I did remove your collar, stupid. And do you realize who's sitting in front of you? I'm not scared of you, Adewale, but please, go ahead, try to use your powers on me. Trust me, sexy, it will not end well for you. Anyways, now that I have your attention, there's something you need to know about your current situation. Because of your actions days ago in Nigeria, and fighting against my friends who I sent here to find Trevyn, you have lost favor with your Queen and the people of Nigeria. They want you dead! The majority anyways. However, what I learned from Queen Aliyu about your little anti-demon tantrum, despite the devastation you caused with your powers, many were injured, but there were no casualties. Talk about getting real lucky.

Adewale: No casualties... so that would explain why I haven't been executed.

Onyx: Not quite, but it did help my case for having her spare your life.

Adewale: What? You're the reason that I have yet to be executed?

Onyx: That is the case, my dear. The next morning while Starfinder was starting Trevyn's training, Queen Aliyu was preparing your execution. Something told me to call her. Right after we talked about Trevyn, I asked her about you.

Adewale: But why? I despise your kind, and yet you cared enough to have my life spared?

Onyx: Like mortals, not all demons are pieces of shit. Despite your actions, I honestly don't think you're really that much of a piece of shit, either. Now back to what I was saying... Queen Aliyu and I got into a little tiff about you, but I was able to convince her to spare you for now. The condition being, of course, is to take you away from Nigeria before the week is out.

Adewale: So, she wants me gone?

Onyx: No, she wants you dead. But... but if you decide to leave Nigeria and *never* come back, Queen Aliyu will, for lack of a better word, "forgive" your actions. That's only if you decide to come with me to Mayland.

Adewale: And do what, serve *you?*

Onyx: That's a privilege you do not deserve. However, there is a place in Mayland for you. New York to be specific. Come with me to Mayland and start a new life or die in Nigeria. It's your call. Should you choose to come with me, if you *dare* target any demon in my country, unwarranted, I will come after you like a lion chases after wounded prey. There will be nothing in this world great enough to stop me from ripping you limb for limb. That's, of course, if you don't choose to stay in Nigeria.

Adewale: I'm not wanted in Nigeria any-more...not alive anyway.

Onyx: So, New York it is, then.

Adewale: What will I do once I get to New York? I don't have any more money, a home, or a job.

Onyx: As if I would just drop you off in New York without a place to live, money in your pocket, or a job that's suited for a man of your skills. I found a nice spot for you in Brooklyn near Utica Avenue. I also have a handsome sum of money waiting in your new home, along with all the necessary furnishings. I'm a King, after all. Anything you feel you're lacking, you can buy with your first paycheck. Speaking of which, you're the newly hired Head of Security at the Prudence High School of Gifted Kids located in Union Square. So, Mr. Osefo, any questions before we get going?

Adewale: Yes... do you need to run any of this by Queen Aliyu?

Onyx: Were you not listening to anything I said? Queen Aliyu just wants you gone. She doesn't care what you do as long as you're not in Nigeria.

Adewale: Then New York it is.

Onyx: See, redemption isn't only for white female characters. Now, Adewale, take my hand as I portal us out of here.

Adewale: Hey, just one more thing before we go...

Adewale reached out to Onyx and embraced him and silently cried on his shoulder. Onyx hugged him back and whispered, "See, I knew you weren't that much of a piece of shit." Onyx opened a portal out of the dungeons of Queen Aliyu's castle and into New York, where Adewale began his new life.

*Darken(s): Humans who are cursed with demonic powers, but they themselves are not demons

ABOUT THE AUTHOR

Onyxe Celestin, writing as Onyxe Blade, is a blogger and YouTuber born in Queens, New York, and is the eldest of four brothers. He's always held a fascination for the unknown. While growing up, he'd often watch cartoons and fantasize about what it would be like to live in such a world. He began creating his own stories in his early teens but, at the time, lacked the confidence to see them through. Now, as an adult, he has the ambition to bring his fantasies to life in book form. He notes Fantasy based stories: *Fairy Tail*, *Queen's Blade*, and *Spectral Force* as major influences in the creation of his FORBIDDEN series.

To learn more about the author, visit his
YouTube channel: Onyxe Blade

To learn more about the FORBIDDEN series,
check out Onyxe's blog:
DarkOnyxe.blogspot.com